My fist cracked the mirror and I watched as a thick pink liquid came out of the cracks and strong winds and smoke entered the room. Objects in the room began circling around me and the wind became more forceful and brought me to my knees. I got back up and touched the mirror, but the mirror started to suck my hand in. I could see a woman's face coming out of the mirror slowly. She had grey long hair and gentle eyes. When she finally made her way through I could see the top of her body and her large biceps. Her entire body was pink.

"It's about damn time!" she said as she grabbed me and pulled me through the glass.

braintown

A novel by

Laura Elizabeth Hernandez

Braintown

ISBN: 978-0-578-43871-9

Email: braintown2060@gmail.com

 Twitter: @Braintown2060

 Facebook: Braintown

 Instagram: Braintown2060

Part

1

Lessons of Braintown

1

Year 2060

I struggled to breathe and my heart raced as I woke up on the morning of my seventeenth birthday. I opened my eyes, and recalled a nightmare I had last night that was equal parts frightening and realistic—the aftershocks were still present. Strangely, though, I could only remember vague moments of being stuck in a place called "Shelatza" and the recurring sound of some creepy but familiar voice chanting something ominous in my ear, over and over again: "Bright, thinking, lively girls with working brains must go away/Shelatza is where they'll be placed/A new type of girl will be molded/The right way."

I got out of bed and my entire body ached. I walked to the kitchen and saw my dad standing there, watching our leader King Manu on the Tellysitter as he does every morning. I've always admired King Manu and wanted to be just like him; I wrote a paper on his dignity, excellence, and character in grades 5, 6, 7, 8 and 9. And I always said that when I got married, I wanted to marry a man just like him. But this morning, as I stared at King Manu on the Tellysitter, I had this sick feeling in my stomach.

"We are all responsible for our own lives and we will not tolerate government-run medical programs," King Manu said from a press event.

King Manu wore a crown made of paper, which had images of himself and the moon. It was green and tall. He wore a gold robe. He stood at 6'8" tall. He had very strong hands. His hands seemed worn but they had grown stronger with each battle.

After King Manu spoke for ten minutes straight—as he does every weekday morning—the Tellysitter cut to a commercial featuring a really skinny, popular model named Gally Bonroe. Gally weighed eighty pounds, had big, wild hair, no pores (and, of course, a fitted bra). I'd seen this commercial a million times, but this morning the commercial made me queasy. I thought, 'It's obvious I have the flu or something because everything is making me feel sick.' I stared at the bones sticking out of her pelvis and as she turned to the camera and said, "Embrace your body! I always do," I felt something come up in my stomach and I ran towards the bathroom and barely made it to the toilet. I threw up everywhere.

I came back to the kitchen and another commercial was playing: this one featured a man buying a woman a Rampurk. A Rampurk was one of the most popular diamond rings on the market and they cost about eight months of any guy's salary. At the end of the commercial the guy gets down on one knee and says, "Julieta Peterson: Will you marry me?" She nods and then they hug. I used to watch this commercial and dream about my wedding day, but today it was up there with King Manu's press conference and Gally—I needed to hold down my food when I watched.

"You look pale—put some makeup on," my dad said as he passed by and saw me staring at the Tellysitter.

"I threw up, dad. I think I'm sick," I said, but he ignored that and went about his business, preparing his suitcase for work.

"It's your birthday... make sure you look good!" he added on his way out.

My dad and I have always been close, but something about him seemed different this morning, too. "No boy is going to want you if you don't," he added. I started to cringe, but then stopped myself: Why were Dad's comments making me feel uncomfortable? He had always been honest with me about my looks and his advice, like, "No boy wants a smart girl" has always helped me in the past. He's a great dad. He loves me. I should listen to his advice and get dolled up for school. *But something is making me sick...*

My dad left a cup and some plates in the sink for me to clean. I didn't use them but it was my *obligation* as a woman to clean them.

I had to head to school soon so I figured it was time to start getting ready. I washed my hair with shampoo, then applied conditioner and made sure to really moisturize the tips—*everyone says this is important.* I applied foam to my legs and grabbed my Shaver 3000. I slowly passed the razor's red light over my leg and watched each small hair on my leg disappear. I did the same thing for my other leg and then I did it underneath my arms. I washed the conditioner out of my hair and applied a special treatment my mom bought me for my hair. It was a honey-looking liquid with no name on the bottle, but she said to apply it to my scalp and tips and leave it on for at least eight minutes. While that was working its magic, I used a very gentle liquid soap that my mom claimed I was *very* lucky to have. It was super expensive. I scrubbed my back with a back scrubber and then cut my toe nails a bit in the shower. Finally, I removed the hair treatment from my hair and turned off the water. As soon as I did I immediately patted my wet body down with a towel because my mom says that air drying can lead to wrinkles.

My mom keeps a long mirror on the door to the bathroom so that I can see what I look like when I get out of the shower. She also keeps a scale on the wall for me to keep my weight stabilized. I stared in the mirror and quickly looked away. I *hated* looking at my body. My thighs touched no matter what I did. I put my full hand on the scale and a robotic sounding voice said, "One hundred thirty-five pounds. Bloating around thighs. Weight increase 1.2% from last reading." I immediately deleted my results so that my mother wouldn't cut my meals in half, or worse, make me starve myself.

I have to do this every day because in my town the only thing that matters if you're a girl is the way that you look.

I stared in the mirror and noticed an enormous zit on my face which I immediately popped. I applied an anti-aging moisturizer cream and a laser which burned a bit but I had to let the light hit every single pore on my face. Once that dried, I put cream under my eyes for dark circles as well as an anti-wrinkle cream. I plucked my eyebrows and applied sun block lotion with an SPF of 100 all over my body to avoid sun damage. I followed up with another moisturizer for my face for dry skin. I walked out of my room naked and stood in front of this large fan and let it all dry. Then I put on my helmet, which blow dried my hair for me, as I did two hundred sit ups on the floor. I got up and removed the helmet, which revealed a bouncy, blow dried look.

I put my fingers in my nail machine and selected the color pink. Ten two-inch nails were added to my fingers and I selected the symbol of a heart on my thumb. That's what all the girls were doing these days. I used the machine to paint my toes as well.

I began putting my face on. I applied red lipstick, made my eyelashes longer, did everything in my power to hide my pores and then added two layers of foundation and a lot of blush with my electronic makeup case.

My mother had selected an outfit for me and left it on the bed. I put it on: a tight cashmere top which revealed a bit of cleavage and a grey mini-skirt. My pumps were black and they had a short heel because my mom already said I'm too tall and that the worst thing a girl could do is make a boy feel short.

I made sure everything was in place so my mother wouldn't criticize me. I looked at myself in the mirror in the bathroom. I lifted up my skirt and saw how fat my legs looked even with my stockings on. This made me angry. I knew my teachers and mom would give me shit for that. I also tried not to think about the stretchmarks I knew were growing on the right side of my thigh. Every day I found a new one because my weight fluctuated so much. I put this special cream on my thighs that is supposed to make my stretchmarks disappear but it never did anything.

My mother helped adjust my shirt in the back and asked me to please suck my stomach in a bit, which I did while I looked in the mirror one last time. "This skirt makes your legs look fat," she said before pulling down my skirt in the back and pulling on the sides to stretch the skirt out.

My mother offered tips every morning on how I could look better, but this morning it took all I had not to turn around and slap her. I felt so much rage as she stood next to me pointing out my faults. But I know she loves me. She wants me to be the prettiest girl in the entire town. She wants me to be pretty so that I will marry a very rich boy who will take care of me. (There was that one time she accidentally electrocuted me in the shower during a makeover...but no one's perfect).

2

RIFF

I stepped out of my house and joined the other girls on my block to wait for the train that takes us to the Institution of Care and Preparation.

"Alice Garcia, you forgot your pin!" my mother yelled.

My mother gave me my pin for the Institution which we all have to wear every day to our classes. No exceptions. As the train pulled up, I suddenly felt very nervous. "GET ON THE TRAIN, GIRLS," RIFF, our morning driver yelled.

I waved goodbye to my mother, who had her usual blank look on her face and never waved back. "Fix the bottom of your skirt," she said as the train doors closed.

We headed toward the Institution. The Institution has an excellent reputation for turning girls into respectable, beautiful and obedient young women who marry rich and powerful men from the Academy of Excellence (the boys' college).

As I sat on the train, I started drawing the legs of the woman I'd seen on the Tellysitter, a woman named Gally.

LAURA ELIZABETH HERNANDEZ

I looked at what I drew. I realized that Gally's legs looked more like arms than legs and her waist was way too small for a normal body.

I looked out my window and saw Gally on a giant billboard looking *even* thinner than in my drawing. Then, I noticed a beautiful butterfly right outside my window.

'Look at all of those colors," I said to the girl seated next to me. "I want a butterfly like that. It wants to come in!" I said.

"Alice, no, just leave the window closed. Come on," the girl said. I leaned over and opened the window to let the butterfly in. It was SO beautiful!

"ALICE! Close that window IMMEDIATELY!" RIFF yelled at me, which made my heart palpitate out of control. "Who told you to do that?! Why are you opening windows?" RIFF asked.

"Oh, sir," I said. I'm sorry. I thought you ordered me to do so. I don't think I slept enough last night, sir. I was doing all of my chores and I'm exhausted."

RIFF— who at 6'8 and heavyset, towered over me— bent down and stared straight into my eyes. My heart started beating even faster and tears started rolling down my face. 'Please don't hurt me,' I thought.

"DO I NEED TO WORRY ABOUT YOU, GIRL?" RIFF asked. I was so scared I couldn't move, let alone talk.

"Um... no, sir. Like I said, I didn't sleep last night while I was doing my required chores. I'm not feeling well. I mean, *good*."

"You're lying!" he said, as he huffed and puffed down over me.

"I baked these cookies for you, sir. I was up late last night cooking for you. I heard you say you loved chocolate chip cookies the other day and I wanted to please you. It was supposed to be a surprise. So when I opened the window, I thought I heard you give me the order and I just wanted to please you, sir."

He grabbed the cookies from my bag and smiled. "Good girl," he said. "I am pleased."

We arrived in the parking lot of the Institution and I saw General XY Harry by the main entrance of the building, waiting for RIFF to drop us off. I walked past him nervously and he stared at me like he knows what I look like underneath my uniform.

"Fix your posture," he said. He took a pull of his cigarette and then flicked it so that it landed right near my foot, but I didn't move. I watched, my hands trembling as he raised the left side of his lip and said, "Aren't you gonna pick that up for me, sweetheart?"

"Yes, sir, of course," I responded quickly. I picked up the cigarette off the floor and reached out to give it to him.

He grabbed my wrist and smiled at me for what felt like an eternity before letting go.

"Now, get in the back of the line," he said.

3

Institution of Care
and Preparation

The Institution of Care and Preparation is a grey, steel building where I spend most of my time. My classmates were lined up in front of the building. At the front of the line were the Dragonflies dressed in their matching outfits: a grey skirt and cashmere cardigan, high heels, and big hair, as required. As we stood on line, General XY HARRY walked menacingly alongside us, threatening us with his eyes and staring at our legs. The look on his face was scarier than the motor-code weapon in his vest.

"It's time. Make your way in," he said. As I walked past Harry with my classmates, I looked to my right and saw the machine that tells us our weight. The machine was also grey and it had two wheels that spun faster and faster as your weight goes up. I forced myself to look and saw the number "130" on the electronic board in front of it.

Once we got to class, Mrs. Ruthberry—my least favorite teacher—was standing at the front of the room in her usual short skirt, grey blouse and shoulder pads with her long legs looking fabulous as usual. On a visual board, the words "HOW TO PLEASE YOUR HUSBAND" showed up on the screen. "All work must be completed in a timely, accurate, and organized manner," Mrs. Ruthberry told us, like she did every day.

Antonia, the most popular girl in school and the leader of the Dragonflies, couldn't be bothered to pay attention just yet. She was Dick's girlfriend and he came from one of the wealthiest and most connected families in town. Being associated with Dick and his family gave Antonia and the Dragonflies certain privileges. Everyone else was obsessed with her for another reason: *her hair*. It was shiny, soft, and long. She loved putting her fingers through her hair. Antonia was the one everyone in our Institution wanted to be and all the guys hoped would move next door. And she took every opportunity to mistreat us all (including the faculty).

I watched as Antonia whispered something to her friend, Penny. Mrs. Ruthberry waited patiently with her arms crossed in front of her body for Antonia to finally join the rest of us. "She doesn't realize she has a fucking hole in her stockings?" Antonia whispered to her friend Jade about Mrs. Ruthberry.

"Antonia, you know we're not supposed to curse," Jade replied. "You're gonna get us in trouble."

"She can't hear me. She's a deaf cow," Antonia said.

Antonia then looked at me and said the same thing, "This moody bitch doesn't even realize she has a fucking hole in her stockings. She's such a disaster."

Mrs. Ruthberry started her lecture: "Okay, young women of Braintown: How do you please your husband at all times? As I've mentioned before, this is a question you'll be able to answer by the end of the semester. It's a big question and a task that not many women are able to accomplish. But I can prepare all the young girls in this room to pass the final exam this year and go on to live lives of service and attempting to please others. I myself struggled to please my husband in the early years of my marriage. I was exhausted. But through inner strength, I was able to meet the challenge. Will you pass the test of your lives as women? It's up to you."

At that moment, Mrs. Ruthberry looked at me. "Alice, what is the most important ingredient of husband pleasing?"

There was still a lot I didn't know about husband pleasing, but I thought about my own mother and responded, "Immediacy?"

"Immediacy is *so* important," Mrs. Ruthberry said. "You don't want to keep him waiting. What else? Let's throw out some other words. I want to hear from everyone."

All the girls began chiming in at once:

"Accuracy," "Attention," "Humility," "Observation," my classmates said.

Jade decided to chime in and really wow Mrs. Ruthberry because she needed to get a good grade in this class and she'd been slacking off lately. "First, I just want to say that I think husband pleasing is not something we should learn in class just to get by. I take it very seriously because I know how important it is. I think the most important ingredient of husband pleasing is absolute submission. You must submit to your husband's dominance and just follow his lead. He will be pleased. I promise you."

"Yes, we discussed that in the last class," Mrs. Ruthberry said.

"And...I just want to add," Antonia said. "That looking real good is very pleasing to his eye."

Antonia's answer made me want to throw up.

Mrs. Ruthberry looked at me. "Alice, what's wrong with you? Are you sick?" she asked.

"No, a little bit. I mean, I'm sorry. Um..." I said. "It's just that I think time for yourself and time to recharge your batteries is important for husband pleasing," I said, without realizing what was coming out of my mouth.

All of the girls looked at me, their jaws on the floor. Mrs. Ruthberry got very pale.

"What do you mean? What are you talking about?" she asked.

I knew I had to think of a quick way to save myself and get all my classmates to stop looking at me. I should 've called in sick. I was *obviously* not myself today.

"I just meant that you'll please your future husband better and be a better wife when he gets home, if maybe you're less tired. You know...because of the energy and attention you can provide."

"Interesting," she said, and she paused. "Men don't like women who think or have attitude problems. The fact that you're even thinking that you should form an opinion on what works for him concerns me."

"But..."

"Alice, let me put it to you in a way that you'll understand. His needs come first and you're there to make him happy and he's there to provide for you and do great things in this town. Understood?"

"But..."

"Shhhh, Alice. Moving on!"

"God, Alice, what *don't* you get? Antonia said. "It's cake, okay?"

What Mrs. Ruthberry said and the way she treated my argument really bothered me. My leg started shaking and the more the other girls looked at and giggled about me the angrier I got and the more my head hurt.

So when she asked again in the middle of the classroom what the most important part of husband pleasing was, I blurted out something I've been doing since as far back as I could remember: "To please someone else you must ignore your own inner voice and live a lie, Mrs. Ruthberry."

Mrs. Ruthberry SPRINTED toward where I was sitting. All the girls stared at me.

"What did you say, Alice?! Look at me! Explain what you just said!"

I immediately felt the weight of disappointing my parents and the disapproving stares of my classmates and knew that I had to save myself from this word vomit. "I don't know what I mean. I don't know anything, Mrs. Ruthberry – just what you teach us. I can't explain it because I don't know what I mean. I just wanted to please you by giving you the best answer I could come up with. I am *so* sorry, Mrs. Ruthberry. I will never do it again," I added.

"I'm tired, girls. Write in your journal application of pleasing ideas while I take a breather. Write about the last man you pleased and how it made his life better. Explain in detail how your assistance took some of the burden off him and helped him accomplish his goals and desires. Submit your assignment to me on the husband pleasing E Drive by the end of the class. No talking."

We all started writing in our Ultrasonic Cognitive Numerical Code Fatherboard Mainframe, UCNCFM. The UCNCFM is where all town data is stored.

I wrote about the chocolate chips I gave to RIFF.

Pleasing Entry 34- E DRIVE Folder

Gave RIFF cookies. I know he really likes cookies and I hope he enjoyed every single bite. Those cookies were made for me and my classmates but Mrs. Ruthberry teaches us that it is better to give what we have to the men in this town, instead of enjoying it ourselves. I know the cookies were delicious and I'm sure RIFF was satisfied after eating them and that made him do his job better.

I swear to live a life of service, always.

—Alice

"I guess it's easy to take it all for granted while you still look the way you do," Mrs. Ruthberry said to me as I exited the classroom. "You're not likable. Work on that. That's your homework."

"I will, Mrs. Ruthberry," I said.

4

The Mirror Room

I walked down the grey hallway and passed all the digital images of women vacuuming while smiling in their living rooms as well as those of girls who had graduated from the program over the years.

I first stopped at my grey locker and typed the name of a man to open my locker. I had to choose the name of a guy I was longing for at the beginning of the year, but since I didn't have one in mind, I just made one up: Javier. I opened my locker and put my heels in there and replaced them with ballerina slippers for my next class. I walked down the hallway and squeezed between two long, grey machines that sprayed a perfume on me that made me smell like a pear. I finally made it to the white door labeled in bright red letters, "Welcome to The Mirror Room."

The Mirror Room was a studio separated by three tall cubes. Each side of the cubes gave one girl access to one mirror. In these mirrors. a girl could see and judge her reflection. There were three mirrors total from smallest (less severe) to largest (extremely severe). This class was considered one of our exercise classes but we didn't actually exercise in it, except for a little stretching on the bars along the wall on each side of the room while we waited for our teacher Mrs. Jackson to call us up one at a time.

I couldn't help but admire Mrs. Jackson's excellent body as I waited my turn. She wore a skintight leotard to class so that we could emulate her almost flawless figure, which she had perfected over the years in the plastic surgery machine. She was still really hard on herself and insisted we do the same.

"Look at the loose skin underneath my arm," she said while she stared at her reflection. "It is not okay. This doesn't look good," she said. "But ladies, remember: These mirrors are not here to harm you. If it wasn't for these mirrors I wouldn't be able to see myself clearly and make the necessary updates and changes to look better. That's what I want for all of you: perfection." She put her hands in front of her and lifted all her fingers up to create a perfect ten. "Do not fear the mirrors, ladies. They reveal the truth."

"Alice, let's go. Get up here," Mrs. Jackson said.

I walked past the purple, red, and yellow cube and found myself completely locked in on both sides with the mirror in front of me. I knew the drill, so I just stood there waiting for "the truth" to be revealed. I could see the zit I sort of finished popping in the morning, and it looked enormous in the mirror.

"Alice, sweetie. What is wrong with your body in mirror 1?" Mrs. Jackson asked.

I walked closer to the mirror to look at myself. I stared at every part of my body as they became just that: parts. As I walked even closer, Mrs. Jackson grabbed my arm and pulled me back. "Don't get too close to the mirrors! Don't *touch* the mirrors," she said. "Now, what's wrong with your body?" she asked me.

"I have a zit on my face and my legs are very chubby," I said. I hated myself for saying it.

"Good."

"But that's all I see wrong with me," I said, wanting to get this over with but knowing that I had to go on to the second mirror.

"Shall we go on to mirror 2, then?" she asked.

"Yes," I said, as I tried to control my right hand from shaking.

I could see all of my flaws even clearer now. "I have thin hair like my mother, and hairy eyebrows which I just waxed. I also have man shoulders."

"What shampoo are you using?" Mrs. Jackson asked.

"Nevianza and a volumizing conditioner."

"Well, keep using it. Shall we go on to mirror 3?"

"Yes," I said.

"I have nasty skin," I said. "My nails are too thin, my feet are huge, my thighs touch. My eyes are crooked and I have deep dark circles under my eyes." The second I said that the mirror made a cracking noise and the bags under my eyes grew six times the size of what they were before. My thighs got bigger and took over the entire mirror and I could see a scar on my legs and the growing stretch mark stretched to the fullest and revealed every thick line. I tried not to cry but it was too much today.

"My ears are too small," I continued. "My teeth are yellow like the sun," I said. Even as I said it, I thought, 'But that last part is not me! At least I don't think it is. My teeth have *never* been that yellow and large in my whole life.

I was ordered to stay looking at my reflection, which had become even more hideous than before. "How much longer do I have to hold on?" I asked.

"Just focus on the third mirror, Alice, for a few more minutes and you're done," Mrs. Jackson said. She put her hand on my shoulder and said, "It isn't easy, but beauty is pain. This is our duty—to look at ourselves in this way. Your future husband, your peers, and any man on the street will be much harder on your body than any of these mirrors I can assure you."

POW! POW! POW! a few seconds of silence and a final, POW!

I looked at the third mirror and something was smashing into it over and over. I could hear a scratching sound and then POW! over and over again. I also heard what sounded like crystals but the sound it was making disappeared so quickly I couldn't make out what it was.

While all the girls got distracted and started running around, I focused on the third mirror and tried to make out the sound it was making. It was like nothing I'd ever heard before.

"Get out of the room, girls! Get out NOW!" Mrs. Jackson said as she wiped down the floor and the pounding got louder. My heart was racing and the sound of the cracking was so loud I feared I would go deaf.

But I couldn't leave her alone. I ran to where she was and grabbed some paper towels from behind her desk and wiped down what I believed to be water—but it was way too thick to be water—with a slight pink tint, coming out of a few cracks that had developed in the third mirror.

"Girls, calm down and stay in the hallway," Mrs. Jackson said.

We all walked outside but I peeked in the room while the girls talked amongst each other. I rubbed my eyes and when I looked again the crack had disappeared and the Mirror went back to normal. The noise also disappeared. How can that be? How does a crack just disappear like that?

"A pipe is broken. No need to worry, girls. Now stay out in the hallway until I finish cleaning this up," Mrs. Jackson said.

The Dragonflies were staring at me when I made my way back to the hallway. I could feel Antonia's intense gaze all over my body. Her gaze felt more like an inspection, like she was trying to decide if the weight of my body, the features on my face, and the bounciness of my hair were good enough for her.

The Dragonflies talked about the pipes and how rundown the school was. "I wouldn't be surprised if one day this building just killed us all!" Antonia said. "This school is so freaking old. I can't believe they expect us to come here every fucking day."

"It has the best traditions and reputation," Jade said to Antonia.

"The best tradition of what? It's about to collapse!" Antonia said.

Antonia was very frustrated by the state of the Institution and had insisted to both of her rich parents that she be homeschooled because she was above it.

Antonia was also the leader of the Dragonflies. I usually stayed away from the Dragonflies or maybe they stayed away from me. But the broken pipe had forced us to socialize.

Antonia raised her eyebrow while she looked at me in the hallway and I noticed she did this for all sorts of reasons. Sometimes it was right when she was about to do or say something cruel. Other times she thought it was sexy, and guys were around, but most of the time she lifted it when she demanded to know something.

"Why are you always so quiet, Alice? Do you think you're too good for us?" she asked me out of nowhere. I was surprised by this question. Me, too good for someone? That thought had never even crossed my mind. But Antonia also had a habit of asking random and totally invasive questions, out of the blue.

"No," I said. "I don't think that at all."

"It sure seems that way. Doesn't it seem that way, Penny? Doesn't it seem like this girl Alice is too good for us. She's just too good to speak to us or just too good to hang with us or just too good to dress like us."

"Yup," Penny said while she played with her hair.

Mrs. Jackson approached us. "What happened, Mrs. Jackson?" Antonia asked very dramatically, like she cared deeply.

"You know what happened, Antonia. This building has been having problems with the pipes for a long time," she responded.

"I know, Mrs. Jackson. And thanks for taking care of everything. You're the best! I mean that. That's why you're my favorite teacher in this *whole, amazing, totally fabulous* Institution," Antonia said.

Mrs. Jackson smiled and walked toward the teacher's lounge.

Antonia pulled me aside. "Come here, you. In all honesty, I'm so confused," she started. "I'm only hard on you because you're pretty and you should hang out with us. You shouldn't be off by yourself." She used her electronic makeup case, the WPX 30XX to apply mascara.

"I need to see your house first, though. How much money does your father make?" she asked me.

Nothing surprised me when I talked to Antonia. She could be very cruel and demanding but this question caught me off guard. "I don't know," I said. It honestly never occurred to me to ask my dad that question, and I felt like a fool for never even wondering. I *do* live there.

"Let us come over," Penny said. "We can try on each other's clothes and do our hair. It will be fun!" she said.

"Yeah. And if you're parents aren't home it's even better. We can just chillax," Antonia said, with a devilish smile.

5

Airhead Home Invasion

Antonia, Jade and Penny arrived at my house at 4:30 BT. "Your parents' room is the biggest, right?" Antonia asked.

I nodded.

"Where's that?" she asked.

"Last door on the right," I said.

Antonia sprinted down the hall to open the door. I watched her open my mom's closet and look at her clothes before pulling out a blouse to try on. She looked at herself in the mirror and decided she didn't like it before putting it back. "Your mom has like no shoes," she said, before running to see the rest of the house.

'No shoes?' I thought. 'My mother has over 25 pairs of shoes!'

She peeked into the kitchen, opened the refrigerator door and then took a look at the back of the washing machine model number. Her inspection had begun and I think she was trying to figure out how much money my dad made by looking at the products we had in our house since I didn't know the answer to her question about how rich my family was. "You know you guys are wasting your time with that washing machine!" she said.

"How so?" I asked.

She didn't answer me.

She walked into my room and headed to my private bathroom.

"Right on! This conditioner is so expensive! Good taste, girl!" Antonia said. "The soap your mom bought you is very pricey, too! But I don't use this one. The one I use is about five times more expensive, but like I said to my mom, 'Skin is forever!'"

I wondered how she knew all of this, but I was beginning to notice that Antonia was like the scanner at the supermarket. She just knew what everything was worth. I guess I never really thought about any of these things as so important. Aren't they just beauty products and machines?

Antonia didn't stop her investigation there. She felt my sheets and said nothing.

"Are those okay?" I asked, not really knowing what I meant by "okay."

She ignored me and then looked at the model of my helmet blow dryer before saying, "Holy fuck, this is the crappiest helmet dryer. Alice, this model is from fucking last year!" she said before forcefully slamming it on the floor. I rushed to pick it up and put it on my nightstand

and sat by the bed. "Can your mother buy you a new helmet? Like, if you asked her would she make a fuss? Does your mom make a fuss in general when you ask her to buy things or is it easy for her to just give you money?" I could see Antonia was still fishing for my value as a person according to my parents' wealth.

"If I need something, she buys it for me. But sometimes she uses coupons. Not always but sometimes," I said. "She says it's good to save when you can and I agree because you just never know in life. Sometimes you're doing well and things are good and you should be thankful, but other times maybe things don't turn out how you planned. My dad works really hard and I wouldn't want to just blow all his hard-earned money. You know, I think we're all very lucky to have all the things we have and I always try to be thankful for it all," I said.

Antonia looked *very* confused. She lifted her eyebrow and walked over to my closet. I couldn't tell if she was thinking about what I just said or if it just didn't go into her head at all. Antonia seemed to have a magnet around her head that blocked out wisdom.

She stood with her arms wide open before feeling the quality of my shirts and pants. I couldn't really read her and I couldn't tell if she was satisfied or disappointed since her face always remained neutral and the only thing she was capable of moving was her left eyebrow. "The quality of these shirts are good, but they're tacky," she said before taking a blue cashmere cardigan from my closet, putting it on, and shutting my closet door. "I'm gonna borrow this. You can borrow stuff from me, too. I'll bring it back next week," she said.

"I don't really like loaning people my personal items," I said, stretching my arm out long enough to get my sweater back. "Maybe I can give you something in here I don't really want anymore. Like this one," I said. She ignored me.

"I need to take you shopping, girl. We'll go next week. What's up with the zebra tights in your closet?" she asked.

"My mom gave me those tights last year."

"Your mom. Aww. You're so cute," she said. She held them up and said, "These zebra tights are not preppy. You need to dress more preppy, girl! Preppy leads to rich guys."

"What do you wear that to, anyway?" Penny asked, wanting to know but not really.

"Like exercising in my..." Antonia cut me off. "Toss them! *Ahhhhhhhh!* I don't want to hear about those tights ever again. They must be destroyed!"

Penny spoke for a second time. It seemed like an inconvenience since she had to stop pouring this tiny colored candy into her hand. She had that box of candy, Goospers, with her everywhere she went.

She said, "I LOVE Goospers and they're only for me! Goospers are wittle like me. I'm so wittle and petite...*hee hee*...I feel like I'm eating little, tiny Penny's," she said.

Antonia interrupted, "Give me some of your sacred Goospers!"

"No!" Penny said; she was bravely protecting her candy. "My Goospers are only for *wittle* people like me."

"Anyway, I don't want your stupid little Goospers," Antonia said.

"What does your dad do?" Antonia asked me.

"He owns a few companies. And yours?" I asked.

"My dad is dead!" she said before quickly turning over on my bed and playing music by DJ Wally, The Love Master, on 76.05.

The hours went by and I noticed that the Dragonflies were deep as a puddle. Which didn't surprise me at all. They talked mostly of boys, money, beauty. With a break period to paint their nails. They used a new app that does it for them.

Penny searched through her bag for her electronic makeup case to show me how to use it better.

"I see you use your makeup case in class and it's all wrong," Penny said, like she was genuinely trying to help me.

Antonia looked kind of out of it. She kept her very large eyes wide open while she stared at the ceiling. She started to play with her black hair while she sang along to the music. "*I love you baby, I do. You make me happy and I'm happy with yooooouuu.* I love this song!" she said.

Penny made her way toward me and she was a lot shorter than me. Penny had the type of look that a lot of guys at the boys' college found attractive. She was planning on perfecting her look by getting F cup tits. She was very petite, skinny and she always smelled like fruits. Today she smells like an apple but I noticed in class she usually smells like a pear, which always make me hungry. She wears a gold necklace that says her name and she is always perfectly dressed from head to toe.

Love songs played in the background while Penny explained to me how to use the electronic makeup case in her hand. Antonia sang along to the hot song, "Nervous."

I'm nervous that you're thinking of leaving
Because without you my heart will never be the same
I can't picture my life without you

"OMG, Antonia. You *sooo* can't sing," Jade said.
"Shut your trap. I can totally sing," Antonia said.
Antonia kept singing in a dreamy romantic tone while she thought of her boyfriend, Dick.

I can't picture my life without you
Pleasing you is all I need

"OMG. I usually don't say this, but shut up," Jade said to Antonia before Penny began explaining to me how to fix my face.

"So, if you want to add foundation to your face, press FP... your skin looks fair so I'm thinking FP394. Yeah, that should work. You have like *really* thin eyelashes. I hope you don't mind me saying that, but you do. Like I'd rather tell you to your face than, like, you know, say something like that behind your back or whatever. But, like, it's okay, we can fix this. So to make them thick and long just like press... I use this key a lot. Press J and 2 at the same time. And for bronzer. Which I think you should use too because it gives you color. You press MJ45. I honestly like *don't know* what color blush you want but I would go with something rosy with your complexion. So press J219," Penny said.

Penny pointed out my flaws like it was a list she was reading off a clipboard. I pointed out all my flaws in the Mirror Room because I had to, but hearing someone else notice all these things about me made me feel really insecure. Could there really be *that much* wrong with me? Could there really be that much wrong with *any* one person? It took me a minute to realize how much everything she said hurt me and how I would never say anything like that to anyone else.

Penny helped me fill out my "inadequate" eyebrows and made my eyelashes longer. Luckily, the chip that was connected to the makeup case was inserted into the back of every girl's neck whether we decided to purchase the case or not.

"You look fucking hot, girl," Antonia said.

Antonia woke up from her romantic coma when she saw, to put it in her words, "how flawless" I looked. "That's how you're *supposed* to look, bitch!" she said to me. She started talking on and on about she planned to marry rich and how she and her boyfriend Dick were destined to be rich and powerful. She gave me a bunch of tips on how to marry rich and how to fool a guy into thinking you actually like him. She stood in front of my mirror on her tippy toes and pulled on her pink lace panties while she stared at her ass. "It's simple. You look hot. When I'm gaining weight, I skip lunch and drink a soda and smoke a cigarette for lunch. Alice, you listening?"

"Yes!" I said, trying to fake enthusiasm.

"If you don't look hot and skinny you can forget about it. Nobody's gonna want to fuck you. And you must hang out with other pretty women. No beautiful woman wants to hang out with unattractive women. Pretty women hang out together. And...actually, wait.

Hold up, I have a zit. *Fuck! Fuck!* What the fuck is that doing there? UGHHH! Why am I getting a zit? Where do zits *even* come from? I look at myself in the mirror and I think, 'Who *am* I? Who *is* this person? Know what I mean?'"

After Antonia popped her zit, she continued. "Anyway, your family has to have money, too. And if your friends also have money: BINGO! You look like you have enough. Then laugh and go along with everything he says. And this is the most important thing: *Never* give him a hard time. *Ever.*"

I started walking around with a garbage can to pick up after the Dragonflies. There were fake nails, eyelashes, hair extensions and all sorts of nasty things all over my bedroom floor and none of them were willing to lift a finger to clean up after themselves.

I was starting to get bored and I was doing everything in my power to stay awake. 'Why don't they just leave?' I wondered.

"Do you want me to shave your legs?" Jade asked me out of nowhere.

"I hate doing it. My legs are so long," I said.

"I'll do it. Come on," she said, as she grabbed my hand and led me to the bathroom.

Jade jumped in the shower with me and softly lathered my legs with soap. She then slowly massaged my legs from the ankle and made her way up to my knee and began shaving with the *Shaver 3000* I use in my bathroom.

"Does that feel good?" she asked me.

"Yes," I said.

"Good," she said and then she smiled and continued shaving my legs. "You have hairy legs," she said.

"I know. I hate shaving my legs. They're so long. It's exhausting," I said.

"Well, I'll come over and shave them if you want," she said.

"That would be great," I said.

Jade smiled at me. "YAY!" she said. "Umm, cool," I responded.

Minutes later, the Dragonflies got bored and took off. 'Finally!' I thought.

6

The Romantic Booth

When I saw the Dragonflies the next day, they were standing together in cashmere cardigans by the Romantic Booths waiting for their turn.

"Alice!" Antonia yelled. "Come here!"

I walked over to Jade, Penny, and Antonia, who all looked genuinely happy to see me.

"So, we were thinking," Penny said. "You can be a drag-along."

"What's that?" I asked.

"It just means you can spend time with us," Penny said. "We like you. You *can't* be an official Dragonfly. It's against the rules. But you can hang out with us because you're so pretty and wealthy."

"Yeah. Sorry," Antonia said, raising her eyebrow. "You have to be a Dragonfly from when you were little. We are friends for life."

'Ok, great,' I thought. Who cares?

But what I said was, "Oh, okay. Drag-along is fine."

They took out their electronic pad and showed me a picture of a dragonfly with 3 boxes around it which contained each of their names. And then a separate box with my name on it. Underneath the box, it read: "Drag-along Alice." The Dragonflies are *very* organized for airheads.

Antonia made a sad puppy face in my direction and Penny followed. "We still love ya!" Penny said.

"Alice, you look like you're going bald," Penny said.

"Bald?!" I asked nervously.

"Yeah, a little up top. We should get her more hair," Penny said to Antonia.

Antonia nodded and Jade chimed in. "I'm on it. I'll get you some. We take care of each other."

We stood by the booth, the latest machine created by King Manu. It was seven feet, five inches tall. He was very proud of it and said so recently on the Tellysitter.

"Alice, your turn," I heard Mrs. Ruthberry say. I put my hand on a pad at the entrance to the booth for vibration wave recognition.

I watched the Dragonflies as they prepared to enter their booths, too. "Welcome, Antonia! Welcome, Jade! Welcome, Penny! Welcome, Alice!" the machines said as we each got shut in.

I sat on my uncomfortable seat as it raised me up all the way to the top of the booth. I saw the name "DJ Wally" in red letters like I'm used to by now. He appeared on the screen in front of me wearing a shiny green helmet on his head.

DJ Wally said, "Hey, Alice. Welcome back to Booth 1! This will be your official booth for the remainder of the school year. Ain't that exciting! You know the rules: The red button *turns me on.* You'll watch me talk and share some videos and you might get a little dizzy sometimes but it's OK! Any questions?" he said.

Before I could answer, he continued. "The door that closed you in should not be opened for *four* hours. See you later, Alice!"

During hour one, he played sappy love songs while I stared at a hypnotic spinning wheel that was black and white. After a while, the colors started to blend into one and my body started tilting over to one side. The blinking bulbs made it even worse and I threw up a little bit in my mouth.

I rubbed my eyes before applying eyedrops to prepare myself to stare at the a hypnotic spinning wheel going even faster in hour two.

"Take a deep breath and hold on tight to the bars under your seat. They will keep you calm," DJ Wally said. "If you reach your breaking point, press the blue button below the wheel. But remember the rules: if you fail to complete your time you will have to make it up again before the end of the month."

DJ Wally continued, "Now, I know you ladies are looking for love! And while you search for the man of your dreams, here's some music to help you hang on to that lovin' feeling! Love is a wonderful thang! The loud music started right away and I covered my ears to protect my eardrums from the song that had been number one on the Braintown music charts for the last few months.

> *I'm nervous that you're thinking of leaving*
> *Because without you my heart will never be the*
> *same*

"I'm so sick of this song," I said to myself out loud.

"Alice, what did you say?" Mrs. Ruthberry asked.

"Nothing," I said. "Great song, Mrs. Ruthberry. I was born to make men happy!"

"That's right!" Mrs. Ruthberry said. "Sing along with the music!"

MISOGYNISTIC VIDEO SHUFFLE
Song: "Attention Hoes"

"Alice!"Mrs. Ruthberry yelled. I can't hear you!"

"I'm sorry, Mrs. Ruthberry," I said.

"Loud enough for me to hear you!"

"Okay, Mrs. Ruthberry!"

I started singing along. "Point out your flaws, bitch. Your only purpose in life is to marry rich."

"Louder!" Mrs. Ruthberry said.

"You're a chicken-head, a piece of meat. HOES DON'T MEAN NOTHING TO ME!'

"Very good," Mrs. Ruthberry said.

SONG: "The Sweet Love of My Life"

I heard Antonia yelling at the top of her lungs in the booth next to me:

I'M EVERYWHERE, DARLING
I'M WATCHING YOU SLEEP
I HEAR ALL YOUR PHONE CALLS
I'M EVEN IN YOUR DREAMS

Next Video: Scenes from *The Little Mermaid*

"Tell me what the message is, Alice!" Mrs. Ruther-berry said.

"IN THE MOVIE SHE LEAVES HER ENTIRE LIFE IN THE OCEAN FOR HIM AND THINKS ABOUT HER PRINCE CHARMING ALL DAY!" I yelled, wanting to get a good grade.

"Very good," Mrs. Ruthberry said. "Continue..."

Next Video: Scenes from *Aladdin*

"IN THE MOVIE HE TAKES HER TO NEW HEIGHTS. SHE CAN ONLY REACH NEW HEIGHTS *THROUGH* HIM. SHE DOESN'T HAVE HER OWN MAGIC CARPET."

SHUFFLE- SHUFFLE

Next Video: Scenes from *Beauty and the Beast*

"IN THE MOVIE AN ANGRY BEAST FORCES A BEAUTIFUL WOMAN TO LIVE WITH HIM AGAINST HER WILL. SHE CHANGES HIM FROM A MONSTER TO A KIND MAN THROUGH HER OWN KINDNESS AND GOODNESS."

I heard Jade explain the movie "Cinderella" in the booth next to me.

Cinderella

"A rich man pulls Cinderella out of her poor exist-ence and the same thing will happen to me if I'm a good person that cleans a lot even when other people treat me badly. In the movie, evil women lose. Good women win," Jade said.

It was extremely hot inside the booth and it shook so much it made me nauseous. As the love songs played over and over, I thought I was going to go insane. After what felt like an eternity, the music stopped and my seat was finally lowered back down to the ground.

"That wasn't too bad, was it?" asked DJ Wally. "I hope you enjoyed the ride. I am DJ Wally and this is 76.05. See you soon, gurlies!"

'Wasn't too bad?' I thought. That was the most painful experience I've ever had.

Mrs. Ruthberry was about to tell us our grades, but something horrible, just *horrible,* was happening to Antonia. Antonia was struggling to get reception to talk to Dick on her Tel-e-kphone. "Dick, are you there?! Can you hear me?!" Antonia asked. Jade and Penny rushed to her side.

"OMG, call him back!" Penny said.

"I can't get him on the line! I don't, like, hear what he's saying and I don't know if he's gonna come over," Antonia said as a tear rolled down her cheek. "DICK! OMG, I just lost the call AGAIN! WTF?" Antonia said.

Both Penny and Jade started crying with Antonia and I scratched my head wondering why. Was it because...forget it. I don't know why they would be crying. Can't she just call him back?

"Just call him back," I said.

"You're so insensitive, Alice," Penny said.

"Insensitive? Just call him back. Dial the number," I said. "Maybe he just lost his reception."

"He's gonna hate me!" Antonia said. "I have to get him back on the line before he forgets about me!" she said in tears..

I've never seen Antonia so out of control and emotional before. It was weird.

"I'll lose so much of my money!" she said. "All my plans are *done.*"

"It's not your fault there is no reception here," Jade said dramatically.

Antonia put the call on speaker hoping it would make it easier for her (and all of us) to hear Dick's godly voice. She finally got him on the line and she let out a deep sigh of relief when he said the words that melted her heart:"WHAT UP?"

"Baby, I'm so sorry. My connection sucks," she said. "Do you want me to come over and give you a blow job later?"

"Yeah," he said and hung up.

"AHHHHHHHHHHHHHHHHHHHHHHHHHHH HHH.   YEAHHHHHHHHHHHHH!   WHOO HOO!!!!!!!!!!!!!!!!" Jade yelled and they all started jumping up and down in excitement.

"You see? You were panicking for no reason. I told you he would want you to come over and suck his dick," Jade said.

"*Whoo,*" Antonia said.

"Don't you think you were all overreacting a bit?" I asked. "I mean, can't you just call him later?"

"Overreacting?" Penny asked. "If Antonia loses Dick, it's over. For *all* of us. You're so dumb sometimes, Alice."

I felt like Antonia had nothing to worry about. Everyone knew men in this town liked having stupid wives they can teach how to think so they can explain the masculine world to them. They also liked having uninteresting wives they can influence and program because they can do whatever they want and still get all of their needs met. Antonia will be fine.

Mrs. Ruthberry had been watching Antonia and all of us with concern in her face. And now that Antonia had finally spoken to Dick and everything was "alright," she told us our grades for our "work" in the romantic booth. "I'm giving you all B's today," she said. "You all did the bare minimum today. Head to your next class."

The Romantic Booth ran extra-long today and sometimes I think they do that on purpose to get us to skip lunch. I was starving.

"Let's go, bitches!" Antonia said while she walked out dancing and singing one of her favorite songs from the Romantic Booth. "I'm a chicken-head, a piece of meat."

"Point out your flaws, bitch. Your only purpose in life is to marry rich."

7

Prince Charming Class—
EMERGENCY SESSION

As soon as I walked into our next class, King Manu appeared on the screen of a large Tellysitter. He began talking and veins were popping out of his neck. "EARLIER TODAY, I RECEIVED ALARMING NEWS FROM MRS. RUTHBERRY," he said. "ONLY THIRTY PERCENT OF THE GIRLS HAVE BEEN PROPOSED TO THIS YEAR AND ONLY TWENTY PERCENT THINK SOMEONE WILL. THESE NUMBERS ARE UNACCEPTABLE AND REFLECT POORLY ON ME AND MY WONDERFUL MACHINES. THIS WILL HURT MY LEGACY. MRS. RUTHBERRY HAS ASSURED ME THAT A NEW CLASS WILL FIX THE PROBLEM INSTANTLY. DO NOT DISAPPOINT ME," he said, before disappearing from the screen.

"I know we can do it," Mrs. Ruthberry said, trembling. "I have faith in my girls."

I was poorly prepared for class and I didn't even have my pink electronic pad. I looked at Antonia and she was busy admiring her own reflection and Penny was extending her eyelashes.

I stared at Antonia while she looked closely at her pores; then pulled out another mirror and looked at her pores from a distance. Then she opened her mouth and stretched her jaw and squinted her eye and looked closely at a pimple, which she popped before smiling at her own reflection in the mirror and putting her fingers through her hair. "WTF, Alice? Why are you staring at me?" she asked.

I didn't realize I was staring at her with my mouth wide open with saliva dripping down to my chin (or that five minutes had gone by). "Oh sorry. Your eyebrows look really cute," I said to save myself.

"Oh, thanks bitch!" she responded, before putting her mirror down on her desk.

A huge, skyward projector was placed in the center of the room and was connected to the UCNCFM. A woman wearing red lipstick, big, thick blonde hair and a tight fitted dress (revealing shiny long legs) walked in and stood before us. It was Gally Bonroe, the model from the billboards around town. I noticed she had no wrinkles at all on her face and she smiled a lot to show off her bleached white teeth.

"Gally is King Manu's #1 sidepiece," Antonia whispered to me. "And she is smokin' hot! I heard Manu calls her over before any other woman. She's so lucky."

"She's a model," Antonia said. "But she's not just a model. She's everything every woman wants to be. She's beautiful, stylish and fun and men want to be around her."

"Hello, girls. Are you excited to be here this morning?" Gally asked in a soft, dreamy voice while removing her white fur coat.

We all nodded and smiled like good girls. All the girls were on their very best behavior because of how good looking our new teacher was. (I guess those things do matter more than I would like to admit). Even I paid closer attention to what she was saying because she's really hot. The hotness led all of us to the false belief that she actually had something of substance to say even though deep down we knew she really didn't.

"Well, I'm happy to be here, too!" she said. "We are gonna get a lot of important work done this morning, okay?"

We all smiled and nodded at the beautiful educator before us.

"Ok, great. Can anyone tell me what a Prince Charming is?" she asked.

"He's a hero!" Antonia said.

"Yes. That's good. What else?" she asked while typing on the keypad connected to the UCNCFM so we could all see the word "HERO" on the skyward projector-optican.

"But *why* is he a hero?" she asked.

We looked at each other not really knowing what to say.

"Well, what makes someone a hero? He has to rescue someone, right? From something bad?" she asked.

We all nodded and smiled.

"What we will be doing in this class is practicing with your Prince Charming to find you yours. He's looking for the right girl to save and it's going to be you this year!" she said as she pointed her fingers at all of us.

"Hell, yeah!" Antonia said.

Gally continued: "A Prince Charming is a very special man. I have my own and he has completely transformed my life in every way possible. This man will lift you up and save you from whatever misfortune you have in your life. But you have to know how to treat your Prince Charming or he'll go away. You don't want that, do you?" she asked us.

"No," we all said.

"Good. You will learn in this class how to speak to your Prince Charming, how to woo your Prince Charming, how to communicate your specific distress without *over-whelming* your Prince Charming. How to make him want you above all the others and most importantly how to *keep* your Prince Charming to become the wife of a citizen. So, who wants to go first?" she asked.

I couldn't get the fact that Gally was teaching us how to secure and seal the deal with our Prince Charming, when she, based on what Antonia told me, was unable to secure the deal herself with Manu. I mean, she had no ring. This little fact seemed to go right over the heads of all my class-mates who wanted to believe everything she said was true and hung on to her every word because she's hot.

Gally asked again. "So, who wants to go first?"

None of us volunteered because we were nervous.

"Okay, I know it's a little nerve-wracking. Why don't we just start with you Antonia since you seem so enthusi-astic," Gally said.

"Sounds like a blast!" Antonia said as she played with her hair to give it some volume before standing in front of all of us. "I love your shoes, Gally. I'm getting them in red next week!"

"Oh, these? Manu got them for me. Aren't they cute. I wanted the one with the buckle but these are cute, too," she said.

"I want the one with the buckle," Antonia said.

Gally smiled and she looked absolutely smitten with Antonia.

"Okay, so let's give your Prince Charming a name...," Gally said.

"That's easy. My love! Dick! Here's a picture of my love," Antonia said as she pulled up a picture from her electronic pad to show Gally. "He's so cute and all man!!!! I just love my baby," she said.

Gally smiled again when she looked at the picture. "You've done very well for yourself, Antonia. I've heard great things about Dick and his future from Manu," she said.

Gally typed in a few codes and a cartoon version of Dick appeared on the monitor with all of the most important information about him on the side:

Future Member of the King's Court
Great financial portfolio
Good family name
Potential Earnings: 600,000,0000 million dollars

"Wow, Antonia. Jackpot! Well done," Gally said. "Now that's a catch!"

"Holy Cow!" Penny said.

"That's my baby. He's so fucking gorgeous!" Antonia said. "I love you and miss you," she said to Dick before blowing him a huge kiss.

"Now, Antonia, to woo and keep your Prince Charming, there are some things you need to know. For example... you never..."

"Oh, please, Gally. I know how to do this. I've been a Cool Girl since I was born."

Antonia slowly unzipped her blouse to expose some cleavage and took a lollypop out of her mouth and began sucking on it slowly before telling a computer version of Dick he was the hottest guy she's ever seen and the most wonderful man on earth. "You're my King!" she said. "Nothing you do is wrong, baby! Nothing!"

Dick blushed and smiled. "Why, thank you."

"You look so sexy in that top. What brand are you wearing? The best, right?" Antonia continued. "You wear only the best! Why don't you unbutton your top and show me what brand you're wearing, Dick?"

Dick did everything Antonia said and when he finally revealed the label Antonia was so happy I thought she was gonna scream. "I knew it! Only the very best for you. But will you buy the best brands for *me* too, baby?" she said as she puckered her lips like a sad baby and her eyes became all droopy. "Will you make me happy, baby? I'll make *you* happy, baby."

Antonia had turned into the superficial, consumer-driven, plastic, brain-dead goddess all men in my town dream of.

"Exactly!" Gally said. Yes! See what she did there? Girls, take notes. That is exactly how it's done. There wasn't an ounce of *inauthenticity* detected by the Prince Charming on the monitor.

Gally looked at me. "Alice... Will you get up here?" she asked.

I got up and stood in front of all the girls as I watched Gally type. All the girls were staring at me and I felt like I was the last person on earth who should go after Antonia. What do I know about a Prince Charming or being a Cool Girl? I mean, I get what Antonia is doing but it doesn't come naturally to me at all. .

"Tell me about your dream man. What does he look like?" Gally asked me.

'My dream man?' I thought, resisting the urge to laugh out loud. "Um... he's tall, has brown eyes and he likes wearing collar shirts," I said.

"Alice needs to make one up because she can't get a man in the flesh!" Antonia shouted.

'I can get a man,' I thought. But I wasn't really sure I could or that I would ever want to because I always associate having a man with cleaning, cooking, degradation, submission, unmet emotional needs, resentment, shallow beliefs, ego stroking, and laundry. And I hate all those things.

Gally kept typing. "Give me a name for him."

"Um... Luis," I said.

Gally typed some more and hit the enter key. A man with brown eyes and a collar shirt appeared on the skyward projector optican: "Okay, say hi to Luis!"

Luis had shiny teeth and perfect shiny hair. I couldn't see anything below his waist but his arms seemed very toned and I could see his muscles through his pressed collar shirt. He was wearing a tie and it was very clear that I would be speaking to a cartoon of a man today.

"OMG, that's so fucking awesome!" Antonia said. "Alice *finally* has a new man! Miracles do happen. I always thought she would be a bridesmaid and never a bride!"

I felt like this was the most ridiculous thing the Institution has made us do. And that's saying *a lot!* I had to fantasize about a Prince Charming/cartoon who goes by the name of Luis. Then I have to mirror what *he* wants in order for him to save me. That's nuts! But I calmed myself down when I realized he had really cute brown eyes and a smile that never went away.

"Hi, Luis," was the most I was able to get out.

"Hi Alice. It's a pleasure to meet you. May I say you look absolutely stunning this morning."

I couldn't help but smile because he was *so* cute and had a sexy voice too. "Thank you," I said.

Was I losing my mind? This wasn't even a real guy.

"Alice, don't just say thank you. Give him a compliment," Gally said.

"Oh, I'm sorry..." I said.

"No problem. That's why I'm here. This is just practice, okay?" she said.

"Okay...Um...You look really good, too. Very handsome."

"Why, thank you, baby," he said.

"I love basketbaltz," he said.

I struggled to get the words out and it felt like someone was burning my jaw as I spoke. "I... L-OVVEE... BASKETBALTZ... UM... TOOO," I said.

"I love movies. Action is my favorite," he said.

I felt myself starting to disappear and my fingers felt like needles. 'I'm not here. I'm fading away,' I thought.

"Relax, Alice," Gally said. "Breathe...You're just having an anxiety attack. Breathe."

I focused on my breathing and was able to compose myself.

"So how can I make your life better, Alice?" he asked.

"Better?" I asked. "I don't know...I don't know what to say," I said as I looked over at Gally.

"Come on, Alice. I'm sure you can think of something," Gally said. Her frustration with me was growing.

"I guess you can make it better by not calling me 'baby.' I really hate it when people call me 'baby,'" I said.

My Prince Charming squinted his eyes before they became watery then lowered his head and spun in the opposite direction. All I could see now was the back of his head.

Gally's face lost all its color as she walked toward me.

The printer by the skyward projector-optican started printing out:

SHE'S TOO BOSSY. SHE'S TOO BOSSY.
SHE'S TOO BOSSY.
SHE'S TOO DAMN BOSSY.

"Alice, you can't be that bossy. Is there anything you want? A bigger house? More outfits? A bigger washing machine?" she asked.

She paused and looked around the room before deciding to talk to me again.

"Now try again," she said before she typed into the keyboard and I watched my Prince Charming turn back around and smile at me.

"Hello again," Luis said. "So, baby. How can I make your life better?" he asked again.

I felt like something was caught in my throat and speaking was this impossible thing I could never do again. I bit my lip before responding. "You can make my life better by... buying me a *huge* house that will be the envy of all the homes in our town. And you can fill it up with amazing, state of the art washing machines," I was able to get out.

"I can do that," he said. "I would love to do that for you."

"I'm sure you could!!!!" I said, sarcastically.

Luis looked sad and disappointed. The right side of the monitor measured my level of attitude and it was off the charts! Gally's machine started going out of control printing the word ATTITUDE over and over in enormous font. Luis looked down and turned his head around again before the skyward projector-optican turned off completely.

Gally was furious. "How *could* you!!!!??????" she asked me. "How could you hurt Luis in this way? Who do you think you are?!!!!"

I didn't know what was getting into me. Was I losing my mind? I touched my head and it was *really* hot and I looked down at my hands and they were shaking uncontrollably.

"Gally I think... I know Alice... and I think she's just having an anxiety attack," Penny said trying to save me. She's not acting like herself."

I could see that Gally allowed herself to buy what Penny was saying because she wanted to believe it to be true. But she continued to stare at me with a cold expression on her face.

"May I get Alice a glass of water?" Penny asked politely.

Gally nodded. Penny brought me a cold glass of water and gently stroked my arm until I calmed down before she went back to her seat.

"Are you feeling better, Alice?" Gally said coldly.

I nodded.

"Good. We must continue. Penny, you're up next," she said.

Penny stood in front of the class and designed her own blonde, blue eyed beauty of a man named Billy.

I found it difficult to focus and Gally noticed right way.

"Alice, I need you to pay attention. This is important. There is no room for troublemakers in my class. Understood?"

"Yes, I understand."

"Penny, please continue," Gally began typing a few things on the keyboard.

I watched Penny do her thing up there and I guess she was doing a good job because Gally kept nodding and smiling in her direction. I thought it was weird she was taking it so seriously. I mean he's not a real guy and this all seems so bizarre to me. She was flirting and complimenting him while stroking his ego for most of the exercise. He seemed to genuinely like her. I don't know why

I'm having all these self-destructive thoughts lately which are making me so do badly in all my classes.

Penny called her Prince Charming Billy and I knew who Billy was and I did remember Penny mentioning him before.

Like Dick, Billy was very wealthy. Billy hadn't asked Penny to marry him because he wasn't all that attracted to her. She found out what haircut he liked on a girl, and she has pictures of his mother to align her look with hers. She also found out that he liked girls with long hair and huge tits. Penny had short hair and small tits. But this is only a small glitch as she planned to make the necessary changes to make her dreams come true.

"Billy, you're so hilarious! You're the funniest guy I've ever met!" I heard Penny say. "Will you help me make decisions? I'm so scatterbrained!"

"Of course. I'll be decisive," he responded. "You won't have to think at all."

"And will I have the nicest mansion in town?" she asked.

"You will and you'll never have to worry about a thing again," he said.

"You're the best Prince Charming ever!" she said.

"Thank you," he said. "See you soon, my love."

"See you very soon!" Penny replied.

Gally started clapping and everyone clapped, too. Even me. I wasn't exactly sure why we were clapping.

"That's how it's done. Great job! I'm glad you went on the first day, Penny. Excellent work!" Gally said.

The bell rang and I grabbed my things. Thank God this nightmare was over!

"Okay, ladies. You're all set to meet the guys! I'll see you all there! Best of luck!" Gally said as she retouched her lipstick. She was *so* hot.

Antonia, Penny and Jade got up and walked out of the room together without me because, as Antonia put it, "I totally sucked balls today."

8

Academy of Excellence Visit

The next day, I met with all the girls in front of the Institution. Mrs. Ruthberry took all of us across the street to the Academy of Excellence for the boys of Braintown. This was the first time I'd ever visited the school. It was *nothing* like our Institution. It was brand new, tall and had a beautiful blue paint coat. The doors were high and appeared heavy and difficult to open. When I looked up at how tall the building was, my neck started hurting. All of King Manu's buildings were an attempt to actually reach the moon because the moon was a symbol of his own greatness.

The boys were outside sitting on chairs from the school. Dick was there and so was Billy. Dick took his electronic board and put the number 7 on it and waved it in the air for me to see. "You're a 7," he said. "You're *barely* a 7!" he shouted again. Billy agreed by nodding and a few of the other boys started barking in my direction.

When Antonia passed by, dressed to impress and in a fitted top and a mini skirt with shiny legs, they wrote another number, a 9 and they began whistling in her direction.

Dick made it to where I was standing and put his face close to mine and began, *"Ruff, ruff, ruff,"* as I made my way to the door. His breath and presence were over me and it felt very uncomfortable, obviously. I don't think anyone would describe that as an enjoyable experience.

"Stop it. Cut it out," I said.

"Ruff!" he said again as I stood by the door. "Now that I see you up close, you're not so bad. You have a nice tight ass and a nice rack," he said. "Come into my school, 7," Dick said.

I didn't know the school belonged to him. "My name isn't 7. It's Alice Garcia."

I didn't say anything else. It was a lose/lose situation no matter what I said. If I said *nothing,* he'd get pissed and if I said *something*, he'd keep going.

"You should say thank you," he said.

I could see General Harry XY♂ watching my behavior and I could see his motor code-weapon on his waist.

I stayed quiet, which is the default mode most women go to when they're surrounded by unfair, cruel forces and have no way to defend themselves. Silence usually works for women. Most of the time.

Penny grabbed my arm. "Isn't that awesome you were catcalled? You're so lucky," she said. "It means he separated you as worthwhile from the pack. Why aren't you more grateful?" she asked me.

'Grateful?' I thought. A guy I don't know invaded my personal space and boundaries, rated my appearance with a number, barked at me and then discussed the beauty of my ass and tits with me. In front of everyone! I can't think of a more uncomfortable situation than that.

The digital screens on the hallway walls lit up with positive messages for the boys:

BE ALL YOU CAN BE
"Nothing great will ever be achieved without great men, and men are great only if they are determined to be so" —Charles de Gaulle

"Lives of great men all remind us, we can make our lives sublime, and, departing, leave behind us, footprints on the sands of time" —Henry Wadsworth Longfellow

I stopped to read the encouraging messages for the boys and I guess I stood there longer than I should have, because Mrs. Ruthberry came by. "Alice, don't read any of that. You won't know what that is. Come on," she said as she grabbed my hand and pulled me back into the group with the other girls.

spacious gym after getting off the elevator. The gym party was made for us to hang out and get to know one another. The gym had monitors of guys playing Fooseball, Basketzballz and Wretzling. The guys were wearing red blazers and creepy smirks on their faces. As I passed them I couldn't help but notice that they only stared at our waists and butts. If they looked at us at all that is. It was clear that they were more in love with themselves than they would ever be with any one of us. Can one of these jerks look at my face? At my eyes? Is that too much to ask?

After getting bored at staring at whatever boring competitive sport they were watching on the Tellysitter and Gally Bonroe in a commercial selling beer where her body was turned into an actual bottle of beer, some of the boys seemed to circle around Antonia. Antonia was a natural with the boys. But it's because she kept it simple and saw things for what they were.

"Do you want my lollipop, Billy?" Antonia said as she sucked on it and put it in his mouth. Billy nodded and even though he knew Penny liked him and she was standing right in front of him, he took the lollipop and put it in his mouth. Dick, who was standing by, gave the appearance of being unaffected by Antonia flirting with Billy for two reasons: One: he's too full of pride to ever show that anyone could hurt him. And two: He liked the competition. Dick slightly shoved Billy, grabbed Antonia by the waist

N T O W N

and started making out with her and grabbed her ass in front of Billy.

Billy, having no one to talk to, grabbed Penny's hand and placed her body on his lap while he watched the Tellysitter. "Penny," he said. "Damn! I have to get a bunch of stuff in order in my locker but who is gonna serve these guys chips and salsa? I told the guys I would do it," he said. He paused and looked at Penny.

Penny said, "I'll serve the guys chips and salsa. No worries."

"You are awesome!" he said.

Penny smiled.

"Can you also wipe down all the counters and clean the cups?" he asked her.

"Sure," she said. "No problem."

"You're the best. Isn't this the girl best?" he asked to no one in particular. "That's wifey material right there." He said it not because he meant it but because he knew it would make Penny eager to please his needs.

Penny lit up. She not only did what he said, but she was thrilled to do it.

After Penny served Billy, she tended to his friends' needs. Which was basically just a foreshadowing of what her life as Billy's wife would be. When he got back from his locker, Billy did us all a big favor. Well, in his mind anyway. He took out his blue electronic pad and read to us passages from his book. He cleared his throat before starting and straightened his back and with an arrogant tone began reading to all of us who had circled around him.

"Her skin was a soft, shiny tan tone. Her legs were like shiny poles that trapped you in their embrace. Her tits were round, perky and soft. But not as soft as her sweet ass which filled your hand in its grasp."

Immediately the girls began complimenting Billy.

"Wow!" Antonia said. "Brilliant! Absolutely brilliant!"

"He's a genius!" Penny said.

I took a seat next to Jade, unimpressed by Billy's book about tits and ass.

"Would you like me to moisturize your legs in the bathroom?" Jade asked me out of nowhere.

"Huh?" I said. "No, thanks."

I looked at Dick while he chugged down a root beer with some shots of whiskey in his cup (which he snuck in) and then proceeded to go to the toilet and pee with the door wide open as girls waited outside the door

"My Dick is cold right now, man," he said. I watched as Antonia waited patiently by the door to have the honor to make out with Dick when he finally stopped peeing.

Dick made his way to where Jade and I were sitting because he decided after his pissing performance that he hadn't talked to everyone at the party.

He put his hand on my shoulder and said, drunkenly, "You look re-ally good...Why... didn't I notice you bee-fore?"

'Yuck' I thought, he didn't even wash his hands.

"I don't know," I said quickly. "You looked really busy."I'm sorry, can you get your hand off my shoulder? It really hurts" I said.

Dick got ticked off by my comment. How dare I have the audacity to *choose* not to flirt with him?

"You aren't even that hot," he said.

I didn't say anything because I was expected to behave properly at the school and all eyes were on me.

"What about you?" he said to Jade. *"Where were you?"* As if to imply that if you weren't near him you weren't really anywhere. Weird.

"I was right here, baby. Waiting for you. I love your shoes and collar top. So hot," Jade said.

"Thanks, baby" he said.

"You totally kicked ass at the Fooseball game. I was cheering for you all the way!" Jade said.

"Repeat. What. I-IIII-II say, Jade," Dick said.

"Sure!" she said excitedly.

"Today is a fine day for play," he said.

"Today is a ... *haha* ...what was it? A fine...?"

"A fine day for play," he said.

"Okay...let me try again: Today is a fine day... for play!" she said.

Jade probably could've repeated the sentence better if she were less self-absorbed. But Dick didn't mind that Jade was pretty and stupid. On the contrary, it made him feel really good. This beautiful girl standing in front of him, completing half sentences gave him the opportunity to be the jerk he really is.

Dick smiled before moving on to other girls. In his mind, he was very special and he needed to spread himself around so that everyone got to experience the magic of Dick.

Jade pulled out a few bottles of whiskey and began drinking because no guy was taking her seriously as a possible, potential mate.

Mrs. Ruthberry, who cared deeply about the suffering of girls without boys, came by and joined me where I was sitting.

"Sit up straight," she said. "Fix your lipstick and eyebrows immediately, Alice Garcia," she continued. "Take out your electronic make up case and fix your face. I can't believe I have to say this. I'm trying to help you but you're such a slow learner."

"Thank you, Mrs. Ruthberry. You're right. I truly appreciate it. You have a heart of gold," I said to earn some points with her.

I hit F9 then Z2, looked in the mirror of my case, watched as Mrs. Ruthberry's grin grew and put my case away. She pointed at her own breasts and told me to adjust mine, which I did. I kneeled down on the chair and adjusted my breasts in my bra to make them look perky by pushing them forward and toward the center. Mrs. Ruthberry gave me the thumbs up. I sat and surveyed the room. It was packed with all kinds of morons. I watched them all drinking and then watched Dick grab a huge container filled with three different beers.

"Chug, chug, chug chug!" the boys cheered as Dick drank from the container.

"Hell fucking yeah! Did I rip this shit or what?!" Dick asked. He finished the container and threw it against a window. The container bounced off the window and fell by my foot.

"If anyone can rip it, it's Dick. This guy's an animal!!" Billy said laughing, which signaled to Penny that she should laugh too at exactly the same moment he did even though she didn't find any of it funny.

"Hi, I'm Eivind," a boy said to me. "Antonia told me your name is Alice."

"It is."

"Aren't these guys a riot?" he asked me. "So much fun to watch."

"Yeah," I said. "And they seem super smart," I added sarcastically.

"You're really pretty," he said. "You look really good."

I didn't say anything. But I did sit beside him with my back straight and my legs crossed because Mrs. Ruthberry was staring at my every move. She nodded in approval when she saw me tight lipped and proper.

"I'm sorry. Did I say something wrong? I didn't mean to offend you," he said.

I hesitated a minute before saying in a voice low enough that only he could hear me, "It just seems like a weird thing to tell someone you just met. But it's fine. Thank you for the compliment," I said.

He looked a little irritated and Mrs. Ruthberry was staring at only me.

"That was sweet. Thank you," I said to him, trying to fix the situation.

He looked around the room for a minute before looking at me again and deciding that I was (compared to some of the other girls) better looking or good-looking enough to give it another try and to stay by my side. "I understand," he said with some difficulty, like he was forcing the words out of his mouth against his will. "You just don't know me yet and don't like being called pretty by people you don't know very well. No worries," he said.

Sensing how difficult it was for Eivind to say those words, I too made the effort to force words out of my mouth. "It's fine. Don't worry about it. Doesn't every girl like being called pretty by strangers?" I answered like any Cool Girl would respond to her Prince Charming.

"I didn't ask about every girl. I asked about you."

"So is that how you decide if you're interested in a girl? By the way she looks?" I asked trying to sound flirtatious even though I was just fishing for information.

"You ask a lot of questions," he said. "I like being attracted to a girl that I want to go out with," he added. "We like your, you know, tits and ass and if you're skinny we like to see what the personality is that goes with the product," he said.

'Interesting,' I thought. That's not how I see myself at all: *a product with a personality attached.*

Eivind looked at me the way all guys look at me. It was with what I call "surface eyes." Surface eyes don't see me, *Alice*, or any girl at all. Surface eyes are skin deep and are trained to look at the size of your breasts, ass, waist and legs when you walk away.Surface eyes always made me feel like I was being looked at but not seen. And it gave me the emptiest feeling in the pit of my stomach. But something in Eivind's surface eyes was a little different from the rest. Something about him made me feel more at

"Alice, what in the f are you doing? Are you tipsy?" Penny said in front of Billy to make me seem normal and cool.

I nodded and smiled. I stared from where I was standing at the electronic board of achievements which had sliding images of Billy scoring a touchdown at a Fooseball game, Dick holding a trophy and pictures of guys debating and giving speeches. It was a school created to fully develop the narcissist within each guy and take it to such ridiculous proportions that he will never have any sense of reality or compassion for others.

"Dick!" I heard Billy say. "The girls are here to play."

"My girl Penny is looking alright these days," Billy said.

I looked at Penny and she looked more than pleased by Billy's 'alright' comment. "Alright?" I thought Penny's starvation diet, fake nails and half a gallon of makeup on her face would get more than an alright from the object of her affection: Billy. But what do I know? I guess Billy had a lot of things about him that would make a woman ignore his indifference to her. He's very rich and he's a bestselling author and entrepreneur.

Mrs. Ruthberry hit the button to go to the 4,555th floor after we all joined her in the elevator. After fifteen minutes in the elevator we all got bored and started yawning. Antonia grabbed onto my arm as we entered a ease with him than with the other guys. So I decided I would try to keep him around.

King Manu arrived to check in on how the courting process was going because it all reflected on him. He walked in with Gally Bonroe on his left and a bunch of women that were too young for him on his right. He was wearing a gold robe.

"King Manu. Thank you for stopping by," Mrs. Ruthberry said. "What an honor."

"ARE THEY ALL PAIRED UP YET?" he asked.

"Most of them are, King Manu," she said.

"GET RID OF THE TWO BY THE DOOR. THE FAT ONES. I KNOW A HOPELESS CASE WHEN I SEE ONE."

"But, King Manu ... I'm sure we can fix them up," Mrs. Ruthberry said.

"THEY'RE A WASTE OF MONEY. GET RID OF THEM. THEY WILL BANKRUPT US. YOU KNOW MRS. RUTHBERRY YOU MUST'VE BEEN VERY BEAUTIFUL WHEN YOU WERE YOUNGER," he said.

"Thank you, your Highness," she said.

"The girl talking to my nephew, Eivind. Who is that?" I heard King Manu ask Mrs. Ruthberry. "Why does she have so much energy in her body? I can feel it from here. Why are her eyes so lively and alert?" I put my head down.

"I don't know baby," I heard Gally say. "She's just a student."

"I don't like her energy. It's rough," he said.

"She's no one. Just another student at the school," Gally said. "She can barely get through her classes. She's nothing."

King Manu looked at Gally's tits and that seemed to calm him down and take his focus off me.

"I'm done here. Let's go," he said to the girls and Gally.

"Do you want to take a walk with me in the garden?" Eivind asked me.

"Are we allowed?" I asked.

"Yes, of *course* we're allowed. We can do as we please at this school. The professors encourage us to be independent and think for ourselves. This is a great school. Shall we?"

Eivind grabbed ahold of my hand without asking and I said nothing to keep up the appearance of a Cool Girl who has no needs or boundaries of her own. We walked to a garden in the back of the school. I took a good look at Eivind now that we were outside and I realized for the first time how good looking he was. He had to be about 6'1 and he has these big strong shoulders and light hazel eyes with perfectly shaped eyebrows. His eyebrows are nicer than mine! He also has big lips and he clearly knows how to dress. He was wearing really expensive pants, the latest shoes and a really cool timesetter on his arm. We passed by statues in the garden and he told me a little about each of them like he was my teacher. "So..." he said. "Do you know much about history? Probably not... This is the statue of the brave Achilles..."

I giggled. "Achilles... Wow. No, I don't know anything at all about Achilles. He looks like a scary and big man."

But I *did* know something about Achilles. I found myself surprised to discover that I knew everything about Achilles. How can that be? I knew he was a Greek hero of the Trojan war and the central character and greatest warrior of Homer's *Iliad*. I've never studied any of this I don't understand. This is not something a Cool Girl would know so I remained silent.

I looked up and saw that the last bird of its kind, The Flotrus Bird, was flying above us. It has beautiful long wings, and a rainbow of purple, yellow, pink and red. 'That's so beautiful,' I thought.

We continued to walk around the garden and he told me stories about all the statues and I pretended like I was learning all of it for the first time even though I already knew what he was telling me.

I could see that Eivind was starting to get an erection around me but he didn't hide it at all. He just kept walking. Antonia was across the garden, giggling with Penny and pretending to have the time of her life (even though she wasn't.) She bounced around and flaunted her fake happiness in a lighthearted way I found nauseating. Eivind looked her way and smiled.

"I love the Dragonflies. Those chicks are so ambitious. They go right for what they want," Eivind said.

'Ambitious?' I thought. I tried to wrap my head around what he said. 'How could he think the Dragonflies are ambitious?'

Eivind took a piece of gum out of his pocket and slowly put it in my mouth. "You have great lips. They're gorgeous!" he said.

I just nodded and smiled and started chewing to avoid saying something I wasn't supposed to say.

A bell rang letting us know it was time to head back to lobby.

"I had a great time!" Eivind said.

"You did?" I asked.

"I would love to see you again," he said as he stared at my breasts. "Would you join me and my parents for dinner next week?"

My instincts told me there was something different about Eivind. That he was simply clueless about how to treat a girl instead of a total jerk. When I looked at him, I thought of an object bending for some reason. I felt like I could manipulate him into treating me sort of okay. Plus, compared to these other losers he seemed like a shining star.

"Sure," I said to dinner with his family.

Eivind smiled, gave me a kiss on the cheek and took off.

I told Mrs. Ruthberry, Antonia, Penny and Jade what just happened.

"That is a *very* big deal," Penny said to me, leaning in for a hug.

9

Plastic Surgery Machines

Today was *the* most important day in everyone's eyes. This was the day you got to look however you wanted for your future husband.

We were told to create three lines near three white machines in the center of the gym. The machines were terrifying to look at. They were long and tightly closed so that you could barely make out what was inside. They also had pictures along the sides.

Picture 1 had the option for B Cup tits.

Pictures 2 and 3-C and D Cup tits.

Picture 4-Supersize F cup tits.

I know Penny had her heart set on Supersize F cup tits and she can't wait to get in there because she knows that's what Billy likes. I know she is also adding some extensions to her hair, which is also what Billy wants and making other changes, too.

Penny was giggling and jumping up and down. She was one of the first to go so she started making her selections. I didn't know why Penny was so eager to make these changes. I thought she was so pretty already. She had the cutest bob, a lovely body and I may be the only one who thinks she shouldn't change *anything* except her personality. "I don't think you need to do all that," I said, as I watched her select everything new, from tits, to her face, to hair, to legs.

Gally entered the gymnasium.

"What's she doing here?" I asked.

"Oh... she told Antonia that she's getting her breasts done and a facelift," Penny said.

"Really? She looks great," I said.

I looked at the tit options but I didn't want any of them. They looked like they would seriously hurt my back and I don't care about the way I look that much. Not enough to change my look.

Penny lay on the bed and a man named Dr. Gilbert strapped her in after she made her selections.

Antonia prepared herself to jump in the third machine and smiled before it closed her in. "Later, ugly bitches!" she said.

Jade made an extreme amount of selections and even Dr. Gilbert suggested she narrow her picks. "Do your legs, breasts, and hair now, and then we'll get to the rest later."

"I don't want to wait. I want it all now," Jade said. "If I don't find a husband soon, I won't have a place to live!"

"I understand," Dr. Gilbert said trying to be compassionate to Jade's struggles.

The beds slid down the auditorium with the three girls on them before they slid into the machines and I heard the doors lock. All anyone could see were laser lights flashing through the tiny opening on the bottom of the machines: blue, red, and then blue again. The machine shook in the air from left to right and I could get small glimpses of the three girls asleep on their beds. It didn't look too bad from where I was standing. It looked peaceful almost. Then I heard a whistle sound and one machine just stopped midair.

"Ahhhhh!!! Ahhhh!!! It burns! Help me!" I heard Jade yell. Her yelling was so terrifying I felt like a fishhook was cutting through me and coming out of my throat and all the hairs on my arms were standing on edge. I could see Jade's face, then her hand covered in her own blood as she smashed repeatedly onto the glass. "Help me! It burns so bad!" But the machine rose higher in the air and shook her from left to right.

Jade didn't stop moving and I saw what appeared to be her leg with her pink sock on it fly past her face and hit the glass.

"Someone please help Jade!!" I yelled.

"OMG!!" I heard a girl say in the crowd. "OMG, blood!!" All the girls started screaming. "Is that blood?!"

Blood was pouring out of the left side of the machine and falling onto Dr. Gilbert and the auditorium. Then it sprinkled in all directions and started wetting everyone, including myself and leaking out of all holes.

Dr. Gilbert figured out how to stop the machine and I watched as it was lowered back to the ground covered in Jade's blood. They opened the container and I slowly made my way to the opening and couldn't believe my eyes when I saw half of one leg by Jade's head, her stomach completely sliced open and her organs pouring out and her nose and eyes smashed in. I threw up and the smell made some of the girls throw up and run out of the auditorium. They immediately tried to bring her back to life which I didn't understand because she was clearly dead. I held her hand while I stared at her hollow eyes before they placed her on a bed and escorted her out of there.

'Where are you taking her? Let me go with her," I said.

"Everything is gonna be okay. Continue with the procedures," Mrs. Ruthberry said nervously to Dr. Gilbert. "We have to get these done today or King Manu will bite my head off."

"This is ridiculous! What did you do to her?!" I asked in tears, surprising myself with courage I didn't even know I had.

They all ignored me and put me back in line with the remaining girls in the gym.

They cleaned up the machine that Jade used and told us all to quiet down and wait our turn. Antonia and Penny were still in their machines getting fixed.

"I am not getting in that thing," I said to the girls in front of me. "Hell no!"

"Alice," I heard a girl in my group say, "You have to. Keep it down. You're making it worse."

"*I'm* making it worse? We all saw the same exact thing, right? You girls want to die here today for some cheap silicone?" I said.

"We need to shut her up now," Mrs. Ruthberry said, looking in my direction. "That girl is always a problem!"

"I'll go in one of the machines now," Gally said. "King Manu is losing interest and I need to freshen up a bit."

"Gally, this time is reserved for our students," Dr. Gilbert said.

"I know. I know. But I'll just be a minute. I messed up. I mentioned a family to the King and he freaked out. He said he can't be attracted to me if I'm even thinking about that stuff. So I think if I freshen up he will forget all that."

"That's understandable," Dr. Gilbert said. "Alice, you're up," he said to me while he adjusted his white gloves.

"I don't think so," I said.

Mrs. Ruthberry joined the conversation. "You don't think so? Get in the machine now, Alice."

Antonia and Penny exited their machines and had no idea what just happened. They were immediately escorted out of the auditorium covered in bandages and Jade's machine was completely cleaned and shut off.

Mrs. Ruthberry phoned in King Manu. "A lot of the girls are refusing to get in the machines because of a tiny error. They're being completely unreasonable."

King Manu showed up on a huge Tellysitter in the auditorium. He looked furious and ready to bite all of our heads off: "THIS IS NOT A MATTER OF DISCUSSION. ALL GIRLS MUST CHANGE THE WAY THEY LOOKED WHEN THEY CAME INTO THIS WORLD. I WANT TO SEE YOUR PLASTIC APPEARANCE IMMEDIATELY AND ANY GIRL THAT FAILS TO ALTER HER APPEARANCE TO WHAT I CONSIDER PHYSICALLY ATTRACTIVE TRAITS WILL BE ARRESTED BY GENERAL XY OFFICERS.

Mrs. Ruthberry and two General XY♂ officers with motor code-weapons attached to their waist grabbed me by each arm while I kicked and screamed. "Let go of me! Don't touch my body! You don't have a right to do anything to my body!" I yelled.

They placed me on the bed and strapped me in. Gally went into her machines as happy as can be. Maybe she was on drugs. She had to be.

"Alice," I heard one of the girls in the group say. "You're gonna get in deep trouble. Just do it. Do you want King Manu to actually show up here with more General XY♂ officers? Come on. Just do it!"

I watched as Mrs. Ruthberry selected C cup tits for me and inner thigh removal.

I slid in my bed down the auditorium (still holding on to hope and goodness somehow) like I watched the other girls do and then watched as the white door locked me into the machine. I felt anxious like I always do in all the machines. I started to see blue and red lights immediately hitting my inner thigh followed by red lasers circling around my breasts. I felt the most burning, horrible pain in my thigh then my nipples before I fainted.

When I opened my eyes, Mrs. Ruthberry was standing there looking at me on the bed and putting bandages around my breasts and inner thighs. "Walk slowly and go to your house," I heard Mrs. Ruthberry say. "You should be fine in a couple of hours," she said pretending to show compassion for me.

I walked as fast as I could to the Mirror Room to see what I looked like but my entire body ached. As I stood in front of the mirror, I removed my bandages and saw deep cuts along my breasts and thighs.

My scars were hideous and my breasts had to be at least a size C. Thank God. I was afraid she would select supersize titties for me. I would never be able to walk again with those jugs. I was angry and felt violated. I felt my fist closing tightly and before I knew it I punched the mirror with all of my might to try and destroy my own reflection.

My fist cracked the mirror and I watched as a thick pink liquid came out of the cracks and strong winds and smoke entered the room. Objects in the room began circling around me and the wind became more forceful and brought me to my knees. I got back up and touched the mirror, but the mirror started to suck my hand in. I could see a woman's face coming out of the mirror slowly. She had grey long hair and gentle eyes. When she finally made her way through I could see the top of her body and her large biceps. Her entire body was pink.

"It's about damn time!" she said as she grabbed me and pulled me through the glass.

Part

2

Shelatza

10

Shelatza

I felt the firmness of her arms around me and it was completely dark. We spun and spun for what seemed like hours, covered in a thick, pink liquid. I felt frozen, but somewhat calm in her grip.

Some time later, I felt the rough, cracked floor below me and realized that I was in a room the size of a tiny closet. 'Where the hell am I? Am I in confinement?' I wondered to myself. 'Am I being punished for my "bad" behavior in the gym?'

I could feel a mouse crawling up my back and climbing onto my shoulder which I immediately threw off my body. I found a bowl of very dirty, warm water which felt chunky but I drank from it immediately because I was so thirsty. I spit some of whatever it was out of my mouth after a few sips because it was so disgusting. It was so humid I found it difficult to breathe.

I started banging on the door. I banged harder and harder until my hand became numb and the mice below my feet started running around my cell nervously. I started to scream for help. "Hello?! Is anyone out there?!" I asked.

"MOVE AWAY FROM THE DOOR," I heard a woman say. I stepped back and standing in the light in the hallway I saw a woman that had to be about as tall as my dad, so I figured she was about 5'8," Her toned biceps and thighs were fully exposed and she had enormous calves too. She was pink and didn't look like the woman that held me in her arms at all. She was slightly younger and she had brown hair. But her biceps were just as big. She grabbed my arm and led me into the poorly lit hallway which was just as hot as the room I was in. I closed my eyes tightly.

'God save me,' was all I could think.

She took me to a room where I saw some old, rusty beds and a bucket of dirty water with a towel by its side.

"Where am I?" I asked. "What are you gonna do to me? Are you gonna kill me? Please don't kill me!" I said. "I'll go back into the Plastic Surgery machine. I'll have my parents pay for the mirrors. Whatever you want it's yours!" I said.

'What does this woman want with me? Who is she?' I wondered. She doesn't look like any woman I've ever seen. If she was going to kill me, wouldn't she have done it already? And why isn't she answering any of my questions? She acts like I'm not even in the room.

The woman grabbed my hands and then looked at my face and my body in the light. She ordered me to follow her and we made our way out a rusty door which led to a beach.

Suddenly I saw the sky above me and it was pink. It was *so* beautiful.

I saw a series of cots hanging from a rope and it seemed like there were women sleeping in the cots.

Two women were fighting with each other as we passed by them and both looked in my direction and then went right back to fighting. They were just as muscular as the woman I was walking with.

"You didn't calculate it properly. Now the foundation will cause it to collapse," one woman said angrily to the other.

"I measured it several times and I can *assure* you that no such collapse will take place here. I am the best architect here and you know it! But if you want to do my job, go ahead!"

"Okay, Asais. You're always right. We all know this."

"I'm not always right. But I'm always right when it comes to numbers," she said. "Mathematics is about accuracy and it's something I take very seriously."

We made our way to a hut at the end of the beach. When the woman opened the door to the hut, I saw the woman who had pulled me through the mirror. She was drinking something out of a small cup and laughing with this woman Asais who arrived at the hut at the same time we did. "Thank you, Cheka," the woman said.

"You're welcome, Ayoka," Cheka said.

Finally, a name to go with the face! I don't understand why she couldn't share her name with me herself.

I couldn't help but wonder why these women look so different from the women I know. And why do they talk so forcefully? I looked around the room for anything that could be used as a weapon but all I saw was the red liquid, which I assume is wine (I hope) in her cup.

"I'm sorry but I don't understand what I'm doing here," I said to Ayoka.

"You're sorry?" Ayoka asked, sternly. "What are you sorry about exactly?" She asked Asais to pour more wine into her cup.

"I'm sorry. Can you please tell me where I am and what I'm doing here?"

"Oh, Alice. You don't know how much it pains me to hear you talking like that." Ayoka looked agitated. "You look terrified," she said. "Doesn't she look like a scared little cat?" she asked Asais.

"Yes," Asais said.

"I'm just trying to understand where I am and what you're going to do with me. Please I'm sorry if I offended you," I said.

"All this girl can say is 'PLEASE' and 'I'm SORRY.' What have they done to you over there?" Ayoka asked.

"Who?" I asked.

"Oh, Alice. There is so much you don't know," Ayoka said.

"Asais, you know numbers better than anyone. I have a little word problem for you. Are you ready?" Ayoka asked.

"Always," Asais said.

"How many times does it take for a girl to apologize for doing nothing wrong for it to equal pathetic?" Ayoka asked her.

"Easy...I would say it only takes one time," Asais said.

"Did you hear that, Alice? It only takes one time."

"But for some reason when I look at Alice I think of the number zero," Asais added.

Ayoka whispered something to Asais in her ear. Asais nodded and then escorted me to the cots where all of the women slept.

I followed a line of rope connecting several balls together in a line. Each ball resembled the shape of a coconut and it had a door on the side for us to enter after climbing a tree beside it. I started to follow Asais up the tree and some girls laughed at me when I slipped on one of the branches but I continued climbing up after Asais. She jumped from the tree to the Ball and asked me to do the same. I landed in a small room that contained a cot with many leaves underneath it and a container of water. 'Clear water! Thank heavens!'

"You'll get used to my designs. I value practicality above all else. You'll be comfortable here," Asais said. "This is exactly to the inch a space designed for your size and height. We will wake you in a few short hours. To bed now," she said before she left.

The cot and the ball I was sleeping in was very small but comfortable. It was just big enough to fit me and it smelled like leaves which almost made me forget how unbearably hot it was.

The heat was so unbearable that it knocked me out immediately.

The next morning, I walked with all of the women who were also leaving their cots and we headed to the beach. They all began washing up in the water so I did the same. I was given a rough straw skirt to wear, a top and a tie also made of straw. I was still healing from the plastic surgery machines so I carefully got dressed and tried to avoid that wounded area as much as possible.

I did notice one girl looking at me and she smiled in my direction.

"I'm Jujuki" she said.

"I'm Alice Garcia."

She stretched out her hand to shake my hand. I shook her hand but I wasn't expecting her to grab my hand so firmly.

"You have such a soft handshake. Welcome!" she said. I know what you are. We've been waiting for you a long time," she said.

Jujuki had one long braid which seemed to start from the lower part of her head but her hair is so long it makes it all the way to the front of her body near her belly button. She also has a pink bracelet that says "Sheltaza girl" on her wrist.

"Waiting for *me*? Why?" I asked.

"Jujuki, stay away from Alice," Asais yelled from a few feet away. "Go to your class. Go think. Put that brilliant mind to work."

"I'll talk to you later" Jujuki said before taking off.

'Why would anyone be waiting for me? What is Jujuki talking about?' I wondered.

A bunch of women were running toward me on the beach. The beach was the first thing to completely take my breath away. It was clear but a shade of pink seemed to come from underneath it. This place is so beautiful but HOT as hell.

I was told to run with the women but they were running so fast I could barely keep up. "If you can't do it get out of the line!" Cheka said to me. "You are messing up our morning routine before class!" she said.

I was trying to keep up but the heat was overwhelming me and I wasn't used to it. I was dripping in sweat and getting a little dizzy. All the women waited for me at the end of the beach and Cheka looked really annoyed.

When I finally got to them Cheka kicked the sand below her feet and yelled something about extra cleaning duty because I slowed them down. "If you can't keep up, you shouldn't join the line," Cheka said.

Cheka shoved me as she walked past me.

I saw a large pink bird (at least I *think* it was a bird) sleeping on a tree. Its wings were protecting its center so I couldn't see much else. But I could see it was very strong and it took up a lot of space in the tree.

"Alice...stay calm," Jujuki said.

"What's happening?" I asked, trembling as the ground below me started shaking.

"Stay calm!" Cheka said.

The ground started to shake more and I lost my balance and fell on the ground and pink drops of liquid came from the sky. The water in the ocean started creating large and loud waves and all of the women around me started to panic.

"What's going on?" I asked, but no one answered. I got up from the ground and watched as Jujuki and Cheka held on to each other. I looked around in search of somewhere to hide. It was my one and only chance to run away from this place.

It started raining a pink liquid from the pink sky and I removed the pink liquid from my face as I ran.

"Where's Alice?" I heard Ayoka say about me. "We *cannot* lose her! Find her now!"

"I'll find her. She couldn't have gone far," Cheka said. I knew I had to run...FAST!

I started to run in the direction of the room I first arrived in. My heart was beating so fast that, after a few minutes, I stopped to catch my breath -- the humidity made it difficult for me to think or see anything in front of me.

"Alice!" Cheka yelled. "Come out! You don't have to be scared." Cheka was completely pink and I could see her large muscles from where I was hiding.

I ran north away from Cheka. I wasn't headed in the direction of the portal anymore but I just wanted to get away from these evil women and I couldn't see much else.

"The Pink Dragon is up," I heard Cheka say. "She'll help us find her. Alice isn't going anywhere!" I looked up and what I originally thought was a bird was four times larger and appeared to look more like a Dragon than a bird. It was hideous: long sharp fangs, pink hair, four long, thick pink tails, pointy yellow finger nails, huge horns above its head and it breathed in a pink liquid which appeared to be warm. It was the most hideous, disgusting monster I've ever seen. Something about the way it looked and moved made me nauseous. It just seemed to knock over everything in its way.

It landed near me and I watched in panic as it devoured everything in sight including worms, bugs and other creatures. It seemed nothing could satisfy this monster's insatiable appetite. 'What a shameless beast,' I thought.

"The Dragon is hungry!" Cheka yelled.

"Good!" Jujuki responded. "I was worried about her. She wasn't eating a lot last week."

These women make me sick.

I watched as Cheka petted the Pink Dragon and both Cheka and Jujuki were still looking for me. The tree, like all of the trees around me, was beautiful. It had different shades of pink and it arched inward before expanding to the pink sky above it. It was covered in a pink liquid and it had a soft, misty pink shadow around it. The trees across from me were larger and brown but the leaves were bright pink and reddish. I could see three pink dolphins swimming together in the water from where I was standing. All the pink trees were perfectly aligned with each other as if they all agreed to do so. The space between them was exactly the same from each other to the inch. "Where is she?

There's only so many places she could be? She's nowhere near the portal," Jujuki yelled to Cheka.

I turned around to run and saw the Dragon staring at me. It licked its teeth and saliva dripped from its lips. 'God help me!' I thought. The Dragon towered over me with its enormous and frightening physique. She breathed out a pink Dragon's breath. which left a bit of pink dust after every breath. The pink liquid she breathed in seemed very warm. I recognized it from the cracks in the mirror room and from the liquid coming out of the pink sky. I closed my fist and prayed "Please God. Help Me! I know you're with me! Please God save me from this beast!"

"It's called Strontium PinkEqualO-T105 in pink liquid forms. It gives the Shelatza Pink Dragon strength," Jujuki said. "It gives the entire island strength."

I was surprised to discover both Cheka and Jujuki standing behind me. "Don't move a lot. Stay still," Cheka said.

"How am I supposed to stay still? If I stay still, it will eat me!" I yelled back.

"You don't have a choice now. If you move she will eat you. She doesn't know you, so moving is not an option," Cheka said.

I ignored Cheka. I ran toward the portal. I felt the Dragon chasing me.

"Are you out of your mind?!" Cheka yelled. "No one runs from the Dragon! Stop running!"

The Dragon flew above me and landed right in front of me again, opened its wings and spit pink liquid in my direction while it circled around me and opened its wings. I grabbed a bunch of pink rocks from the floor and held them in my hands.

"What do we do?" Jujuki asked Cheka.

"Nothing now," Cheka said.

"We have to do something," Jujuki said.

"Just stay quiet," Cheka said.

I stayed firm as the Dragon made its way closer to me. It smelled my hair, my arms and then it looked right into my eyes. Its wings opened wide again in front of me which multiplied its size by eight. It was the most hideous thing I've ever seen. "Despicable, disgusting, monstrous beast!" I yelled.. "Is that why you both brought me here? So that I can be eaten by your Dragon?" I asked Cheka and Jujuki. "Is that why you took me from my home?!

"Stay calm," Cheka said. "Stop making noise. Let the Dragon become comfortable with you."

"I don't want to play your game. I want to get out of here. Just take me to the portal. I want to leave," I said.

"That isn't an option, Alice. Just stay still," Jujuki said.

The Dragon lifted its wing high and patted my head. She did so very quickly before extending both of her wings as high as she could and flying away.

I was relieved. "Thank you, God!"

"But once you get to know her, she's not so bad. She doesn't really bother us and we don't bother her," Jujuki said. "Ayoka likes to say the Shelatza Pink Dragon grew from heartbreak and disappointment. The kind she felt after something terrible happened to her and we all landed here. And if that's the case, there's no way she'd ever hurt any of us."

"Come with us, Alice. We're not going to hurt you," Jujuki said.

I started running in the direction of the portal again.

"She's heading for the portal!" Cheka said. "I can't believe this crap!"

"Stop her!" Jujuki said.

"This is your fault. We should've grabbed her when she was by the Dragon," Cheka said. "Asais and Ayoka will not understand any of this. Not finding Alice and bringing her back to class is NOT AN OPTION."

I couldn't find the portal. I thought it was north and everything seemed to be as I remembered except for the portal. I don't know if I'm at the right place. I looked up and the only thing I could see was the flying Dragon. It looked me straight in the eye. It opened its wings above me and stayed in place as it flapped.

"She must be below the Shelatza Pink Dragon," Cheka said. "Hurry!"

"Leave me alone! You're a bunch of cruel and scary women! I don't understand this world you live in. You can't make me stay here!" I yelled. I knew they were coming right for me.

"Cheka, we know where she is but if we do it this way, it won't work," Jujuki said.

"You were wrong the last time," Cheka said.

"I know. But I'm not wrong now."

I could see Jujuki coming closer to me holding something that appeared to be a tambourine. She stood in front of Cheka and started playing it before handing her one, too.

"What's the point of this?" Cheka asked.

"Alice has a joyous spirit," Jujuki said.

"How do you know that?" Cheka asked.

"I can feel it. She's just scared," Jujuki said.

"This is ridiculous," Cheka said.

"Just trust me," Jujuki said.

Jujuki started playing the tambourine and so did Cheka. They passed the tambourine back and forth to each other in a fun and happy way. Then Jujuki played the tambourine louder for me to hear. "Alice, come out. I know you're scared. I know what they did to you. It's okay here. You can come out of hiding," Jujuki yelled.

I had no choice and the sound of the tambourine did make me come out from behind the pink tree.

"Give us a chance," Jujuki said.

Jujuki handed me the tambourine. "Have you ever played one?" she asked.

"No," I said.

"I played the flute once. But only for a bit."

"Well, here we don't play the flute. We play the tambourine," she said.

"Follow us," Jujuki said.

"I'll follow you if you start to give me some answers," I said.

"I'll do my best to answer your questions when I can."

"You're just going to have to trust me," Jujuki said.

I was terrified. But I followed Jujuki and Cheka back to the beach. What choice did I have? There was nowhere to hide. They took me to a classroom nearby.

When I got to the class the desks were in a circle and I sat in the only open seat close to the window. I was glad to sit there because it was so hot! I noticed there were quotes on the walls.

"Figure out who you are separate from
your family, and the man or woman you're

in a relationship with. Find who you are in this world and what you need to feel good alone. I think that's the most important thing in life. Find a sense of self because with that, you can do anything else." — Angelina Jolie

"You could certainly say that I've never underestimated myself, there's nothing wrong with being ambitious." — Angela Merkel

"A woman is like a tea bag – you never know how strong she is until she gets in hot water." — Eleanor Roosevelt

Asais stood in front of the class and introduced me. "As everyone can see we have a new student. Her name is Alice." No one reacted to the introduction and Asais quickly began her lesson.

"Two large and 1 small pumps can fill a pond in 4 hours. One large and 3 small pumps can also fill the same swimming pond in 4 hours. How many hours will it take 4 large and 4 small pumps to fill the pond?" Asais asked.

Everyone raised their hands immediately before Asais chose Cheka to answer the question. "T = 5/3 hours = 1 hour 40 minutes," she said confidently.

"Is that right?" Asais asked.

"Of course, it's right. When am I wrong?" Cheka responded.

My heart was pounding so fast in my chest and I quickly started writing down the questions Asais was asking and tried to keep up.

"A rock is dropped into a water well and it travels approximately 16t2 in t seconds. If the splash is heard 3.5 seconds later and the speed of sound is 1087 feet/second, what is the height of the Well?" Asais asked.

All the women raised their hands so quickly again. Asais made her way back to where I was sitting. "Alice, please answer the question," she said.

I looked back up at the board and started writing very quickly in my notebook and suddenly the number 178 came to mind from out of nowhere. "I think... I'm not sure. But I think it's..."

But Cheka interrupted me. "178 feet to the nearest unit," Cheka said while rolling her eyes. "Jesus. Is this girl for real?"

I was right. It was 178. But how did I know that? My heart was racing so fast.

I tried to talk to some of the women in my class but they seemed as frustrated with me as Cheka was and even though the answers seemed to come to mind as Asais asked the questions, I just couldn't get it out of my mouth.

Class ended and I saw Jujuki's smiling face across the room. "*Psst.* Let's go. Let's get out of here!" she said. "Let's go to the beach. It's only your first day. Things will get better."

She extended her hand and I put my hand in hers and she escorted me to the beach. We got there and sat on the sand together. She pulled an orange looking juice from her belt and handed me one. I took a sip and it was really strong and bitter tasting.

"It's alcohol," Jujuki said. "It's my creation. It's called Tiqui-Tiqui Juice. I made it in the lab at school," she said.

"What's in it?" I asked.

"That I can't tell you. It's my own creation," she said. "One time I created a drink so strong that I fainted as soon as I drank it. It was great! But my inventions are more important to me than anything. It's a small price to pay in the name of science! The one I gave you is light. I have them in order from lightest to strongest on my belt. See?" She showed me the order on her hanging belt.

"Everyone here seems to love science and math," I said.

"Yeah," she said. "How can you not? It's so much fun! But we love everything. We're very curious women."

"So are you an inventor?" I asked.

"I guess. I don't like labels. Everyone here is this or that. I've never been that one-dimensional. I'm more of a generalist. I like a lot of things. Know what I mean?"

"Yeah. That makes sense," I said.

"Jujuki, why are all of the women here pink?" I asked.

Jujuki smiled. "When a woman is fulfilled and happy she turns pink," she said. "Her skin just lights up! It's an expression of our incredible power as women."

"Will I turn pink?" I asked.

"If you want to, I guess. You should. It's awesome!" Jujuki said. "Come on. Follow me. The water is so beautiful."

Jujuki grabbed my hand and we ran into the water together. The water felt perfectly warm and clear and I could see a pink tint in the sand below me. "This is the most beautiful beach I've ever seen," I said.

"Look at the sky. Isn't it great?" she said.

"It is. It's unbelievable," I said.

"Jujuki, where did you go? Jujuki?" Someone pulled me underwater. I looked around and saw Jujuki smiling in her pink form in front of me and the pink tint made her look brighter. Then we both resurfaced.

"Why did you do that?" I asked.

"Lighten up," she said before she splashed me.

Jujuki took something out of her belt. It was a bracelet like the one she was wearing. It read, "Shelatza girl."
Then she smiled. "I am making you an honorary Shelatza
girl," she said.

"Thanks," I said.

I finished what was left of my Tiqui Tiqui juice and
headed back to my cot.

It was really hot, but the sky, the water, the trees, the
sand, everything smelled and looked fresh and clear. It's
everything I always imagined paradise to look like. And
there was a pink light that stretched across the sky which
gave the clear beach beneath it the most beautiful glow I'd
ever seen. I couldn't stop obsessing and staring at the
beautiful pink around me.

11

Instinct

The next morning, I ran with all the girls again including Cheka, but this time I kept up with all of them just fine. I started running faster than ever and passed them all and even left Cheka behind. I was starting to get used to the heat or maybe the anger was fueling my fire today but I didn't question it. I just ran. When I got to the end of the race I thought Cheka would be thrilled since it meant that we wouldn't have to do anymore chores and I didn't slow down the line formation. I looked at her and smiled but she still looked annoyed and frustrated. She put her hands on her head in frustration and kicked the sand below her feet before storming off.

'Great! What did I do now?' I thought. But I didn't have much time to think about it because we had a math class to get to. I brought a notebook and a pencil with me.

Asais immediately began her usual Q &A period:

"A woman is walking along a straight road. She notices the top of a tower subtending an angle A = 600 with the ground at the point where she is standing. If the height of the tower is h = 25 m, then what is the distance (in meters) of the woman from the tower?" she asked.

All the women raised their hands and of course Cheka raised it before everyone else.

"14.23," Cheka said confidently.

I couldn't help but think Cheka was wrong. Based on my calculations I got 14.43 and I think I may know where Cheka made her error.

"I'm sorry, Cheka. That is incorrect," Asais said. "Anyone else?" She looked around and all the women started writing in their notebooks trying to figure out where apparently all of them had gone wrong. "Alice, what did you get?"

I was so scared to talk and I didn't even know why. "I... um... I think it's... I think I know where Cheka went wrong," I said.

"Just tell me the answer, Alice," Asais said. "It's not that complicated. Either you know or you don't."

"I can't," I said. And I really couldn't. Nothing was coming out of my mouth. I felt so intimidated by the strength and confidence of the women around me. I was also trained not to talk my entire life.

Asais went to the board and wrote the correct answer: 14.43. I guess I was right and now I was terribly embarrassed and my face turned red.

All the girls were ignoring me except Jujuki and I had all that I could take of their constant stares and eyerolls. I got up from my chair and stormed out into the hallway.

"Alice, where are you going?" Asais said. "You can't leave class until 20 minutes to 4. We have important work to do. This isn't a game."

But I didn't answer her and I didn't care. I just wanted to go back home. I couldn't believe I was actually even missing my electronic Prince Charming, Mrs. Ruthberry, and Antonia. I was so incredibly homesick and *hot!* And here I'm taking crap for no reason and no one will tell me why.

Jujuki joined me in the hallway and placed her arm around me. "Everything is gonna be okay. You just have to give it time. You just got here," she said. "You can't be this thin skinned in life."

"I want to go to my house. I want to sleep in my bed. I don't get what anyone wants from me here and I can't give it to them. Nothing I do here is good enough."

"You're just over-thinking everything," Jujuki said. "The next time someone asks you a question, don't doubt yourself. Just answer the damn question. You can do it. I know you can do it," Jujuki said.

"You don't know anything about me, Jujuki,' I said before storming off to the beach, staring at the sky and breathing in and out slowly. I felt the worst pain in my abdomen. Ayoka came out of her hut and saw me standing there alone holding on tightly to my stomach.

"What are you doing here? Why aren't you in class?" she demanded to know.

"Because I want to go home," I said.

"Well, that's not an option. And you don't really want to go home. You're running away from something," she said.

"I'm not running away from anything. I don't have to do anything. I'll take my evil town over a bunch of cruel, lying women," I said.

My stomach was in so much pain and I was having a hard time breathing.

"Alice, come into the hut to rest," Ayoka said.

"Oh, do you all of a sudden care about me?" I said.

"I've always cared about you. That's why you're in Shelatza with me now."

I hesitated at first because I had developed a deep dislike for Ayoka and how she treated me. But I did what she said because I needed to get out of the heat and lie down. I put my hand on my stomach and focused on my breathing.

Ayoka took a wet a piece of cloth and put it on my head. "I know it's not easy. Letting things come to the surface," she said.

Ayoka grabbed my hand tightly before continuing. "Your mother never saw you, did she? For who you are. The town didn't see you either. You cared for the world and what do they see when they look at you: objects and parts. I know your pain all too well."

My body tightened and became contorted. I covered my own mouth to stop from screaming because the pain in my stomach increased.

"Don't push it down. When a woman's soul cries it's not hysteria. Cry, scream. But don't push it down. Bite me. I don't care. Just don't push it down. We're not in Salem, Massachusetts," Ayoka said.

"Alice, what do you want? Tell me your truth."

"I *don't* want to be put in my place

I want to be selfish

I want to be funny

I want to be free

I want to be loud

I want to punch, kick and scream

I want it ALL

I WANT POWER

"Alice, no one can have it all, sweetheart. But that's good," Ayoka said.

"Why is that good?"

"It's good because it's your truth," she said. "Without truth evolution is not possible. Truth is the key to everything."

"I feel so guilty," I said.

"Don't. These are all good things. This is your truth," she said. "We share the same truths."

Ayoka then hugged me the way a mother should and in a way my own mother never had. It felt foreign to me and I just wanted to run from her embrace. But the more I tried to pull away, the tighter she locked me in her arms. "It's okay, Alice. I knew you would be complicated," Ayoka said.

Jujuki entered the room.

"Alice! Come over here!" she yelled.

"What is it?" I asked.

"The Shelatza Pink Dragon! Look at her!"

I looked over and she was having so much fun alone. She was flying up to the sky, extending her wings and then flying back down. She stopped on the beach and ran closer to the ocean and then ran back.

"OMG, this never happens, Alice!"

"What?"

"This means she wants someone to join her on her journey in the pink sky. That's how she lets people know they are welcome. She's usually a diva so this never happens!" Jujuki said. "I'm gonna go. You can watch," she said.

"Wait..." I said. I couldn't believe what I was saying. "If it's okay with you, I would like to ride the Shelatza Pink Dragon."

Jujuki nodded.

I walked closer to the Shelatza Pink Dragon and felt her scaly skin. It was warm. I looked at her sharp and long teeth before feeling her wings. When I did she tightened a bit so I patted her wings and that relaxed her.

"Hurry up. Jump on already! You're taking too long," Jujuki said.

I didn't realize I was talking so long. "It's just... Well it's quite an animal to look at up close." I jumped on the dragon's back and she immediately opened her wings. All of a sudden and without warning, the Shelatza Pink Dragon lifted me toward the pink sky and started going faster and faster before taking one dip then two dips. The humidity seemed to go away at this altitude. I grabbed on harder to both sides of her as she increased her speed and I could see below me Jujuki waving to me and I could also see pink animals in the ocean. I felt the Dragon's weight below me and it felt strong and safe. The Dragon kept me on my toes. I thought she was going left and then she would decide to go right. Then she would go down and then climb back up. "Holy! Moly! Jujuki! Faster! Higher!" I yelled.

"Faster! Higher!" I demanded before it dipped down and went above the clouds and I could see all of Shelatza.

"Come down, Alice!" Jujuki said.

"I don't want to!" I said. But the Shelatza Pink Dragon did.

The Shelatza Pink Dragon landed in front of Jujuki and squatted in front of a tree. I slowly got off of her and ran to Jujuki who hugged me. "Are you okay? It's fun, right?"

"Yes! That was the most fun I've ever had!"

"Your face is so pink!" Jujuki said.

"Do we just leave her here?" I asked Jujuki.

"Yeah. She's fine. She's resting. Come on. We have to go back to class."

12

Origins

I went back to class. After Cheka gave me a death stare, I gave her one right back and then she turned back around to face the board as I opened my notebook.

"Welcome back, Alice," Asais said.

"Thank you. I'm happy to be here," I said confidently.

I was able to follow Asais easily. She wrote the following problem on the board: "$\log 5x = \log (2x + 9)$"

"Anyone want to take a stab at it?" she said.

I immediately saw the number 3 in my head and blurted out "3."

"That's correct!" she said. "And what about the next problem. Anyone?"

Solve for x the equation $\log_x(8e^3) = 3$

"2e" I said. "X=2e."

"That's correct also. Good," she said with a look of joy on her face. "Let's try a problem slightly more challenging."

"What are the maximum value and minimum values of $f(x) = |2sin(2x - pi/3) - 5| + 3$? I'll give you all a few seconds to figure that one out," she said

"The maximum value of f(x) is equal to 10 and the minimum value of f(x) is equal to 6," I said.

"That's correct, Alice," Asais said, smiling.

"This girl is ridiculous," Cheka said.

Cheka stormed out of class and slammed the door on her way out. But I didn't care and I even enjoyed getting under her skin. It gave me a weird high I've never experienced before.

Asais walked over to where I was sitting. "Good work today. Meet Ayoka in her hut seventeen minutes to five," she said.

"Yes, Asais," I said.

When I got to Ayoka's hut she seemed happy to see me. "Please come in, Alice. Sit next to me."

I sat on the rough chair that Asais was sitting on when I first met them both.

"I heard you did better today. Did you realize your abilities with numbers today?" she asked me.

"I think so. I didn't know I could solve complicated math problems in my head so quickly. I mean, I kind of knew. I see the answers in the form of pictures," I said. "And I guess I kind of always have."

"I have no doubt," she said. "I think during your time here your abilities will continue to surprise you Alice. I know how tough you are even if you don't just yet. Let's get out of here and take a walk."

I didn't understand how Ayoka knew so much about my abilities or why I should trust her at all.

I followed her out of the hut and we walked together along the beach. It was still pink and unbearably hot as always so we both wet our arms and legs with the water of the ocean.

"It's almost 106 degrees Farenheit today," she said as she wet her legs. "It just keeps getting hotter. I'm afraid for the women. I'm afraid for myself," she said.

"You don't seem like a person that gets afraid of anything," I said.

"Well, I'm glad it *seems* that way," she responded. "Some people are better at hiding their fears than others, I guess."

"Why is it so hot here?" I asked.

"Shelatza is scheduled to burn... I don't know how to say this exactly and it's going to sound very strange to you so please bear with me. You are the one who will save thinking women and take them back to Braintown," she said, looking at me with a great deal of compassion in her eyes. "In two months Shelatza will get so hot it will be impossible for any life form to live here. We need to get out of here as soon as possible," she said.

"But what does that have to do with me?"

"You will learn more during the next few days. For now I will tell you that I created you and you were destined to go through that mirror the exact moment to the minute you went through it."

"What do you mean you created me?" I asked. "How could you have created me? From what?" I asked.

"From the Universe," she said.

"From the Universe?" I asked.

"Yes. From a mathematical equation. I will help you realize you incredible mental abilities to go back to Braintown and prepare you for the mission ahead. It won't be easy, Alice. It's serious work and it's an enormous risk I'm asking you to take. You will work harder than you've ever worked in your entire life. I promise you that," Ayoka said. "And you will just have to figure a lot out as you go along. Which is why I made you so practical, logistical and a great problem solver. I don't have all the answers for you but I have a few."

She paused before continuing. "There is a Brain. A center. Which was created and designed by Asais and exploited by King Manu with misogynistic codes and messages," she said.

"The Brain controls and manipulates all the girls into submission. The Brain also controls every machine in your town. If you don't destroy it, all the other machines could simply be replaced and do what they were created to do," she said. "But you must destroy each of the other machines first.

After you destroy the brain you must then smash the glass ceiling with a code. By smashing the ceiling, you will open the portal and get us all home. People will then be free to choose. They will have free will to decide how they feel about us."

"But I don't have any weapons. I have nothing. I get in trouble in Braintown for speaking and thinking. They'll destroy me," I said.

"No, they won't. And you do have a weapon: Your incredible brain."

"But why me?"

"Because you are the only one that can, Alice. The only way to destroy a town controlled by a Brain is with an exceptional brain that functions mathematically," Ayoka said. "And that's the kind of brain you have; computational, high-order cognitive, and mathematical."

"Yeah, but why not Jujuki or yourself, or anyone else for that matter?"

"Because I can't. They can't. I created you for this purpose. I created you between dimensions so you can travel back and forth. In you is the power of the entire logistical Universe. You are not from my body or your mother's body. You were created from the Universe using mathematics. In your body lies all the power, strength, determination, wisdom and intelligence of women and it came to you from the Universe. You are a mathematical equation."

"You're telling me I'm not human? My parents are not my parents? I'm a mathematical equation."

"Yes. The mathematical equation made the neurons of your brain come alive. You can do anything, Alice Garcia. You just have to picture it with the immense power of the Universe. Picture it and it is yours to solve. With your brain you can make any version of the Universe come alive. There's no problem too great for you or obstacle too large. I'm sending you back through the portal in fourteen days."

"What is the mathematical equation that created me?" I asked.

"You know the answer to that," she said.

I paused. I *did* know.

$\underline{F}$

ST=4000bnNEURONS=P1000FS   (W+mt+90%E)
_Seven *By Jerk Standards=AG

F IS FEMINIST ST IS STRONG P IS PICTURE FS IS SPEED W IS WOMAN MT IS MULTITASK E EQUALS ENERGY AG EQUALS ALICE GARCIA

LAURA ELIZABETH HERNANDEZ

"Asais made you a seven according to jerk standards of beauty ideals in a hyper patriarchy," Ayoka said.

"That's what Dick called me. A seven."

"You *are* a seven. According to shallow standards of beauty and the weird numbering associated with sexist thinking.' We had to make you a seven because if you're a perfect ten, people tend to nod along and agree with whatever you say in a hyper patriarchy that values beauty over brains and if you are below a seven they tend to claim that you're only fighting for equality because you're unattractive. It's stupid and awful but we don't run the world. We have to play by their rules to win," Ayoka said.

"Alice, I should warn you. Courage in a woman is hard for some people to handle. They may throw you in jail. But you have to get us out of here."

I hadn't realized how stunning Ayoka was. I mean, she wasn't like the girls back home. She wasn't small and soft. She had big, strong legs and arms and she was very tall. Her face was also very sharp along the jaw lines and her eyes were big and open with thickly shaped eyebrows but she definitely caught your attention when she walked into a room. Seeing her like this made me want to be physically strong for the first time in my life.

"I want the girls of Shelatza to prosper in Braintown and they can't do that the way that town is currently set up," she said. "Girls in your town will never stand a chance as long as all those machines are operating. They will remain stupid, shallow and braindead while King Manu is still in power. It will also make women like you and me outsiders and radicals to the state."

We will continue our discussion tomorrow," she said. "Asais is waiting for you. Go!"

13

Mental Energy

Asais rushed to our classroom with a bunch of papers under her arm. I walked in and saw one empty desk in the class in front of the board.

"It's just you and me today," she said.

I sat down next to Asais. She put a helmet on my head and looked at some numbers on the side of it. "Think about anything," she said. "Anything at all."

I thought about Albert Einstein, Susan B. Anthony, Cervantes, Abraham Lincoln, clean water and Joan of Arc.

"Okay, very good," she said. "A lot of mental energy. Slightly more than I expected, actually."

Asais continued: "Alice, stare directly into the glass in front of you. What do you see?" she asked me.

"Scrambled symbols, codes, pink lights... oh, wait... I see King Manu," I said.

"Anything else?"

"I see Ayoka by his side. And you by Ayoka's side. Is Ayoka Manu's wife? Is she a Queen? Why is she sitting by his side?"

"Yes," Asais said. It was a time when women had to marry the men they wanted to be. Ayoka wanted to be a leader so she married King Manu," Asais said.

Suddenly everything got really dark.

"Wait... are you still in the room? Asais, can you hear me?

Flashback through Alice's helmet: 2040

Queen Ayoka and King Manu are being interviewed by a reporter:

"Well, it seems you do a great job of governing with Ayoka as your cheerleader," the reporter said.

"Well, I know it seems that way. But Ayoka has much less to do as Queen than I do. Obviously," King Manu said. "So she has more time to perfect the work she does than I do."

Ayoka laughs it off.

"You don't seem like you want to sit back and enjoy your role as Queen. Why not kick back and relax?" the reporter asked.

"I guess I could do that, but I like to play an important role in this Administration. I care deeply about what happens to my people," she said.

"Most Queens in the past have been comfortable in their supportive role to the King," the reporter replied.

"Well... If I can help and be of service to my King I think that makes things better for everyone in town,"

Ayoka said. "I'm currently working on two proposals: One to give women the rights to their own body and the other to ensure all of the citizens of Braintown have proper medical care."

"Ambitious," the reporter said.

"Asais and the Shelatza women have backed me on this, so it's only a matter of time before the King comes around as well."

"We'll talk about it some other time," King Manu said dismissively.

The reporter and King Manu look uncomfortable.

"So medical care will be your top priority King Manu?" the reporter asked.

"It will be my issue," Ayoka said. "I already told you that, among other things. I also want to focus my attention on education as well for men and women," she said.

"Alice, are you okay?" Asais asked me through my helmet. "You're sweating. Do you need a break?

"No, I'm fine," I said.

"Okay, we're going back," Asais said.

The King's Gala:

I could see the Gala Room in my helmet. The King and many of the Shelatza women were there. The Shelatza women were grouped together chatting among themselves. King Manu's entrance was welcomed with applause. Ayoka strutted and there was a lively expression to her eyes. She seemed to notice everything through those big, wide eyes and they carried a sparkle of wisdom. Everyone got up and clapped when she walked in. They seemed to really love her.

When Ayoka sat next to King Manu she immediately got down to business. "So what are the updates on my proposals? When are you signing them?" she asked. "I've been waiting a long time."

"Ayoka, this is not the time to discuss this. We have guests," he said.

"But it seems to never be the right time for you," she said.

Ayoka drank wine from her cup and asked Asais more about the proposals. "They're ready on our end."

"Did you hear that, Manu? They're ready," Ayoka said. "I know you're busy outlawing the wearing of mustaches because you don't like them or telling your Generals XY♂ to imprison people because you have a mood swing. But this is important to me... You can't just walk around treating people in this vicious way."

"I'll be back," King Manu said as he walked over and started talking to his guests. He paid special attention to Gally Bonroe.

"Today's your birthday!" Gally said. "Let's celebrate!" She smiled, which revealed her bleach white teeth that matched her white evening gown.

Gally stood up in front of everyone at the party and declared:

"He's so incredible! So unstoppable! He's my King! He's the one and only unstoppable King Manu!" She giggled and drank champagne. It was obvious Gally was on heavy drugs. But no one seemed to notice or care about her health at all. Why would they? She was so beautiful.

"*Ha!*" King Manu said. "What a gorgeous lady. Absolutely stunning."

Gally giggled again.

"That was the most disgusting thing I've ever seen," Jujuki said to Asais.

"I agree," Asais said.

Gally and King Manu walked out of the hall laughing together arm in arm in front of everyone. Asais followed them to a bedroom and found Gally and the King making out on a bed.

"How predictable," Asais said.

King Manu didn't seem that upset. Gally picked up her bag, wiped her mouth and walked out of the room.

"As always, Asais, you can't seem to keep your nose out of other people's business. This has nothing to do with you," he said.

"Embarrassing my Queen has everything to do with me. You humiliate her. You humiliate me," Asais said.

King Manu grabbed Asais' arm. "Are the machines set up for the codes I want to insert?" he asked her.

"What are you using them for?"

"That's not your concern," he replied

"I think I have a right to know what you're doing with machines I designed and created. You're going to use them to control the public, aren't you?" she asked.

"What I do with my machines is not your concern," he said. "And I don't answer to women," he said, storming out of the room.

"Alice, are you okay?" I heard Asais say. "You look really pale. I'm taking off the goggles."

"Just give me a second," I said.

"Do you need a break? Let's take a break from the helmet," Asais said. "You should understand your brain. By my calculations, your brain works 1,000 times faster than the normal brain. Your brain is not a normal brain. You can retain more information than average. Anything and everything you see your brain will store as a picture and information you need will become available to you in the *form* of pictures."

Asais drew a picture of something very familiar to me. I recognized it before she finished her drawing. "The Romantic Booth!" I said without realizing how excited I was to see something familiar from back home.

"Yes. The Romantic Booth," she said. "The codes on this machine were created to keep girls in your town in a dreamlike state, dreaming about boys and going boy crazy to avoid thinking about their own ambitions."

"I know," I said.

"The code to destroy this machine is on the right side of the board. Please take a picture of it with your mind so that I may continue."

I looked at the code in a shape of a boy and a girl for a split second and took a picture of it before she erased it. She told me to put the code back up on the board from memory, which I did:

@Romantic FANTASY – BOYCRAZY -+ BOYCRAZY + FANTASY desktopcopy%romaticreg + **VIRUS DETECTED** + FANTASY + **WHILE YOU WERE SLEEPING** ++ FANTASY MAN + HOW DO I LIVE WITHOUT YOU_ **UNREALISTIC EXPECTATIONS of LOVE** + EMPTY FEELING WITHOUT HIS GAZE- *(y+penisenvy)* + **BREAKFAST AT TIFFANY'S** + GHOST ++/mlong-ing/fclose_(heart_break////(80) *CINDER-ELLA__ PRINCE _*THE WEDDING SINGER + CHARMING---- DISNEY____snow white - ARIEL NO VOICE - BEAUTY AND THE BEAST- batscopy Wire + WHEN HARRY MET SALLY ++ R + Booth. /**PSHUTDOWN** _ ANNIE HALL +

SLEEPLESS IN SEATTLE + + **RSHUTDOWN** + **R SHUTDOWN** +%%calctskill + iexplore + R +Pretty WOMAN ++ **SHUTDOWN** +R **SHUTDOWN** + / @RO-mantic + *HEAT* + THE WAY WE WERE +++_____RTERMINATION//+++Want.What.You.C An.T.Have. UNREALISTIC EXPECTATIONS

2060.relyonhimgray///

2060.relyonhimgray////

2060.relyonhimgray///+*"nonamegirl"*

I also took pictures of several other codes. One to ter-minate the electronic prince charming, the plastic surgery machines, and the mirrors in the Mirror Room. I took a picture of the Mirror Room code:

@Mirror + *SELF* + HARDEST _ON_SELF - **no inner beauty** MSHUTDOWN. WIRE. CALCIEXPLORE-**BEAUTY SKIN DEEP_** UNREALISTIC STANDARD OF BEAUTY- MSHUTDOWN- Monster Reflection----**TOO THIN**< M SHUTDOWN M **TOO FAT**----M ROOM **THIGHS TOUCH**- M ROOM- **HAIR TOO THIN**- **BUTT TOO LARGE**--M I EPLORE SHUTDOWN -DESKTOP- **FEET TOO BIG** -- **EYES TOO SMALL** - **INSUFFICIENT EYEBROWS** -- SHUTDOWN -**NOT ENOUGH. TOES TOO LARGE**--

NAILS TOO THIN---INSUFFICIENT- (--innerbeauty) ????!! INSUFFICIENT -- INSUFFICIENT- INSUFFICIENT- NOSE TOO LARGE - EARS TOO POINTY- INSUFFICIENT =INSUFFICIENT- HATE SELF- HATE REFLECTION- EAT LESS- *DISTORT IMAGE - DISTORT IMAGE - DISTORT IMAGE –* FUNHOUSE - FUNHOUSE - SHUTDOWN -M SHUTDOWN - DESKTOP

And of course the Prince Charming:

@Hero+Thinking for You _ SAVE ME! SAVE ME! SAVE ME! *Cinderella* + Eric+ No Voice _____ The LIttle Mermaid -++++ Desktop +++++ Cool Girl &&&&&& PRINCEM SHUTDOWN ....THE BEAST____*Aladdin can show you whole new world*++++DESKTOP ----- ROBIN HOOD SAVE ME! Desktop SHUTDOWN

"We will go over how to destroy the Brain closer to your departure date," Asais said.

"Okay," I responded, out of breath.

14

Pink Warrior

I found the other girls by the area by where we sleep. Cheka and Jujuki were eating cacao and talking about something but I couldn't make out what from where I was standing. When I walked over I could feel a cold and hard stare from Cheka as usual. Doesn't she get tired of hating me?

"Where you been?" Jujuki asked me.

"With Asais," I said.

"Doing what?" Jujuki asked me.

"Preparing to go back home and some other things," I said.

"And some other things?" Cheka said. "You don't have to be coy with us. We know exactly what's going on."

"Great! That saves me the trouble of having to explain it all," I said.

I reached over for some wine. As I started pouring, Cheka took the cup from my hand. "That's not for you," she said.

"Oh... I thought this was for everyone," I said.

"Well, you thought wrong," Cheka said.

"Come on Cheka. Cut it out. Everyone can drink the wine," Jujuki said.

"Cheka, what is your problem with me? I feel like you've had it out for me from day one," I said.

"I don't care about you at all," she said.

"Well that much is obvious. But why?" I asked.

"You think you're better than everyone," she said. "And you're not."

'I don't think I'm better than everyone. Why does everyone think that?' I wondered.

"Cut it out, Cheka. You're acting like a bully," Jujuki said.

"Just because Ayoka has some fascination with you because you can finally get rid of King Manu doesn't mean that all of us have to like you, too," she said.

"I'm not asking you to like me," I said.

"Please, that's all anyone's been asking us to do since you got here. But Ayoka has to take responsibility for the situation she put us in," she said.

"Cheka stop," Jujuki said. "Don't go there."

"What?" I asked.

"We wouldn't even be here depending on a coward like you if Ayoka had better sense. And I'm not gonna kiss your butt and you're not drinking my wine!" She pulled the container further away from me. "Ayoka should've been bold and taken King Manu down herself."

"Cowardly? Is that how you see me?! Give me the wine!" I reached for the cup and Cheka's hard fist hit my face. She pulled me down by the arm to the ground and began kicking me.

"Get off of her, Cheka!" I heard Jujuki say. "She is the key to getting us out of here. Have you lost your mind? We'll die here!"

I closed my fist and punched someone for the first time in my life. I punched Cheka right between her eyes and knocked her out cold.

"Wow," Jujuki said. "That was awesome!"

Jujuki helped Cheka when she opened her eyes and got up from the ground. Cheka refused to talk to me from that point forward. I tried a few times but she was determined to hate my guts. So I just let it go. But if she wants to fight me again I gladly will.

But I had more important things to worry about than Cheka. I spent most of my time talking to Asais and going over the codes.

15

Departure

I woke up on the day of my planned departure for one final meeting with Ayoka on the beach.

Ayoka sat next to me as we stared at the beautiful ocean.

"I guess I should tell you where you were found when you were born," she said.

"Where?" I asked.

"They found you by the mirrors in the Mirror Room. Can you believe that was the first room you were in?"

"I think that's kind of funny," I said.

"Why is that funny?" she asked me.

"Because it's the room I hate the most in the whole town. There is nothing I hate more than looking at my reflection in the mirror. I can't think of anything less interesting, narcissistic or shallow," I said. "Especially when that image is distorted to make me hate myself."

"I understand, Alice. I wanted to be the one to deliver the last code to you myself," She said before she showed me the most complicated code inside of pictures:

- BRAIN-GIRL-*CONTROL*-BRAIN- LIMITS ####
DESKTOP # VIRUS # ***DESTROY*** _UNLOCK/ALL THAT
MATTERS ARE A WOMAN'S LOOKS--Woman is a misbegotten man and has a faulty and defective nature
in comparison to his. Therefore she is unsure in herself. What she cannot get, she seeks to obtain through
lying and diabolical deceptions. And so, to put it
briefly, one must be on one's guard with every
woman, as if she were a poisonous snake and the
horned devil. ... The word and works of God is quite
clear, that women were made either to be wives or
prostitutes. *–Martin Luther* #PROTESTANT
REFORMERS SEXISM. SERVE OTHERS - *BOY CRAZY-*
--- BOY CRAZY---PUT SELF LAST____ %%%% **VIRUS**
____DESKTOP____DESKTOP_____ **VIRUS** //////
3:12 PRESS MiSogyny Marie Antoinette Let them Eat
Cake ++HATED QUEEN_++*GIVE US AN HEIR* Women
ARE DEFORMITIES_ ARISTOTLE ------ FREUD #####
PENIS ENVY --- SUBSERVIENT ----NEVER PRETTY
ENOUGH %%%%%% THIGHS TOO BIG---- VIRUS----
DESKTOP----NOSE TOO LARGE #### VIRUS ///self-
less///SELFLESS ---BODY NOT WHOLE---BODY AS
PARTS...Euripides+++*No woman is a genius; women
are a decorative sex*++++OSCAR WILDE#####*"If
[women] become tired or even die, that does not matter.
Let them die in childbirth–that is why they are*

there."++++MARTIN LUTHER ------"Woman is made to submit to man and to endure even injustice at his hands." Jean-Jacques Rousseau. "Women are nothing but machines for producing children - NAPOLEON++++" DESKTOP__ VIRUS *-3:16 Unto the woman he said, I will greatly multiply thy sorrow and thy conception; in sorrow thou shalt bring forth children; and thy desire shall be to thy husband, and he shall rule over thee. The male is by nature superior and the female inferior, the male ruler and the female subject.* **OPEN**----WOMEN FREE----NO LIMITS---- VIRUS DESKTOP++*Woman is a temple built over a sewer. – Tertullian ##### DESTROY###* VIRUS ----For it is improper for a woman to speak in an assembly, no matter what she says, even if she says admirable things, or even saintly things, that is of little consequence, since they come from the mouth of a woman. *–Origen (d. 258):* Fragments on First Corinthians. ####*The feminist agenda is not about equal rights for women. It is about a socialist, anti-family political movement that encourages women to leave their husbands, kill their children, practice witchcraft, destroy capitalism and become lesbians. —* Pat Robertson, Southern Baptist leader #Why exclude women? *...Because their delicacy renders them unfit for practice and experience, in the great business of life, and the hardy enterprises of war,*

as well as the arduous cares of state. Besides, their atten-
tion is so much engaged with the necessary nurture of
their children, that nature has made them fittest for do-
mestic cares. John Adams *(Women Have the Right to*
Work Wherever They Want, As Long As They Have the
Dinner Ready When You Get Home John Wayne//
*()#####*Nature intended women to be our slaves... they
are our property; we are not theirs. They belong to us,
just as a tree that bears fruit belongs to a gardener...#Napoleon///= It is the law of nature that
women should be held under the dominance of man.//{}
Confucius <A proper wife should be as obedient as a
slave Aristotle _____Men are governed by lines
of intellect — women: by curves of emotion." James
Joyce*>?_ The education of women should always be rel-*
ative to that of men. To please, to be useful to us, to make
us love and esteem them, to educate us when young, to
take care of us when grown up, to advise, to console us,
*to render our lives easy and agreeable.... #*Rousseau "Finally — woman! ()One-half of mankind is weak, typically
sick, changeable, inconstant — woman needs a religion
of weakness that glorifies being weak, loving, being humbled as divine. "Friedrich Nietzsche

"I can't remember all of that," I said.
"Yes, you can," Ayoka said.

Ayoka looked destroyed. Like she could barely find the strength in her body to tell me another story, but she did anyway.

"I thought King Manu only partially hated me and the women of Shelatza. He certainly put on a very good act of at least pretending to tolerate the work that we were doing but as our power grew, he grew meaner and colder. On my last day... I'm sorry..." she said. "Go put on the helmet and have Asais show you. I think it will be better for you to see it," Ayoka said.

I ran to the classroom in search of Asais. I found her there with the codes. "Ayoka said you can show me what happened," I said.

"Sit," Asais said.

She put the helmet on me again.

I felt the tight, uncomfortable helmet on my head and focused on the pink lights which eventually spread around the edges and created a strong enough light for me to see what was happening.

FLASHBACK: 2040

"Get up," I saw a General XY♂ soldier say to Asais who appeared to be sleeping.

"What?" Ayoka said while she rubbed her eyes. The General XY♂ soldier grabbed her by her hair and pulled her down the hallway. Other women were screaming as well and their screams sent a terrifying shock through my body.

"Get off of me!" I heard Ayoka say. "Respect your Queen!"

Jujuki jumped on the back of the man dragging Asais and bit deeply into his neck.

Cheka was fighting off two men at once and she punched one right between the eyes. They both grabbed her while she kicked and screamed down the hallway.

"Stay calm!" Asais said.

"Fuck you!" Jujuki said to the man who grabbed her by the arm and pulled her hair.

"Alice, are you okay?" Asais said.

"I think so," I said.

I focused back into the helmet and saw all the Shelatza women in a prison cell.

"Don't panic," Asais said to the Shelatza women including Ayoka who sat separately in a prison cell nearby.

"How can we not panic?" Jujuki asked while she put a cloth around her mouth to stop the bleeding.

A General XY♂ soldier angrily opened the door and hit Cheka on the side of her head.

"I demand to know why I was thrown in this prison cell," Ayoka said.

"Your demands don't mean anything anymore," the General XY♂ soldier said.

"Where is King Manu? He will get us out of here," Ayoka said.

"He'll be here soon," the General XY♂ soldier responded.

King Manu walked in and looked at the Shelatza women in the prison cell. Ayoka looked at King Manu with a pained look in her eyes.

"You're going to get rid of us?" she asked.

"Ayoka, you know me so well," King Manu said. "I think you've all caused enough trouble. Wouldn't you agree, my love?"

"If you do this, all of the work I've done for Braintown will be gone. All the progress I've worked for. You couldn't possibly do what I do because you don't care about the people at all," Ayoka said.

"Well... we will have a different Braintown now, I guess," King Manu said. "But Ayoka, you're so naive. It amazes me that someone as brilliant as you can be so stupid. You actually *believe* in progress. In making things better. Destroying the progress is the entire point. *Destruction* is the point. I don't let anything move forward. I keep things stagnant. The fact that you would ask me that shows just how naive you are about the way the world works." He drank a little bit of whiskey he carried by his waist before grabbing on to the prison bars and looking at all of the Shelatza women and saying:

"BRIGHT, LIVELY girls with working Brains MUST go away, In a man-made portal. It's the only way. Shelatza is where they will be placed. A new type of girl will be molded the right way!" EXPIRATION DATE 20 YEARS AWAY."

As soon as he finished, a strong wind entered the cell and blue lights surrounded all of the women.

Everything turned blue in my helmet and I took the helmet off and looked at Asais.

"He betrayed Ayoka. He betrayed you all," I said to Asais.

"He did more than betray us, Alice. He destroyed everything that mattered."

All of the women showed up at the classroom and we all walked together through the woods that I had originally walked through when I got here (we even passed the prison I was locked in).

"I'm sorry about what Manu did to you. It was cruel," I said to Ayoka.

"It was. But Alice, don't be naive about the world you live in. I was, and it cost me big time."

"Are you ready?" Ayoka asked me.

"Yes, I am," I said.

"Put your hand on the wall of the cave softly. You don't need to apply force," Ayoka said.

When I touched it, the cave wall started to melt like the mirror back home and I immediately knew what to expect.

Ayoka and Asais looked at me with hope and concern in their eyes.

I looked up and saw the Shelatza Pink Dragon flying above me with her wings extended and free as a bird. As free as I wanted to be.

I could feel the force from the wall sucking my hand in and before I knew it I was gone into darkness and pink lights. I tried to stay calm as I went 'round and 'round with the little bit of pink light around me providing some comfort. It was much scarier this time because I was alone. The spinning got faster and faster and I closed my eyes tight and blacked out.

Part

3

The Pink Revolution

16

Surprise

When I woke up, I was back in the Mirror Room at the Institution of Care and Preparation. I looked in the mirror and saw my distorted reflection which gave me huge hands, big eyes, and pale skin. I immediately remembered just how much I hate this stupid and evil town.

"Alice! For God's sake. Where have you been?! We've all been looking for you for hours since your procedure!" Mrs. Jackson said as she stormed into the Mirror Room.

'Hours?' I wondered to myself, confused.

"What's that on your face?" she asked.

I looked in the mirror and noticed a large, pink rash on the right side of my face. It seemed to resemble the pink Shelatza sky. I tried to rub it off but it wouldn't come off.

I walked to my house and for the first time since my surgery, I stared at my new breasts. They had mostly healed but my nipples looked like frozen raisins. I stopped staring when someone knocked on my front door.

I looked through the peephole and there was a girl standing there but I didn't know who she was. I opened the door and noticed she had a huge basket with a bunch of pink stuff in it and a teddy bear. She smiled at me and I smiled back. "Can I help you?" I asked her.

"I came to see how you're healing," she said.

"I'm feeling better," I said. "And you are?"

"You're so funny. It's me..."

"Me? Am I supposed to know who you are?"

"Are you serious? It's me... Penny."

"Penny from the Dragonflies, Penny?"

"Yes, dork!" she said.

I couldn't believe it. Penny was *unrecognizable*. She had huge breasts and was at least two inches taller. Her teeth were glossy white and her ears were smaller. She changed the color of her eyes to brown and her hair was so long it passed her new smaller ass. But she still smelled like a pear and she was chewing on her favorite candy so it had to be her. I wasn't completely convinced though, so I tested her before letting her in.

"Give me a Goober," I said.

"Hell, no, bitch," she said. "They're only for petite, *wittle* people." And after she said that I let her in.

"My breasts hurt so bad I just want to rip them out," she told me. She sat on my couch slowly. "My back is killing me. I can barely sit up right now," she said.

"What size are they?" I asked.

"They are the super tits. F cup titties! I've wanted them my whole life. They are *all* I've ever wanted," she said and then forced a smile on her face.

"Penny, why did you do this to yourself?" I asked. "You were so beautiful the way you were."

"Are you saying I'm not beautiful now?!" Penny asked.

"No. I just mean you looked fine. You looked like *you*."

"Yeah. Well, Billy loves the way I look now," she said.

"I'm sorry. I'm just in shock. You don't look anything like yourself at all."

Penny struggled to swallow before continuing. "I have a ruptured disk in my neck and the nerves are pinching at the spine and I'm having severe back problems with my muscles on my right shoulder..." she said trembling as she grabbed a warm glass of water that I didn't notice was just left sitting on my table. She continued. "I'm in so much pain... and my spine..."

"It's okay. Slow down. Take your time," I said.

"Thanks... and my... spine is being pulled for (she stopped to swallow) ward from the... from the weight of my breasts. I've had numbness in my arm from pinched nerves so my arm has been going numb on and off since the procedure."

"How much do they weigh?" I asked.

"Three pounds. They are 650cc's in size. Dr. Gilbert recommended I go down to at least a D but I feel like I'm gonna hold out and see if my pain goes down a bit. Billy really likes it."

"Well, if Billy likes it then I guess the excruciating pain is okay," I said.

"I'm surprised you didn't get more done. It was all free," she said.

"Maybe some other time," I said.

Penny handed me a gift basket, which contained rosy tissue paper, toilet paper, ribbons, sheets, and a bracelet.

"Penny, this is so thoughtful and sweet," I said.

"I know you're a drag-along and Antonia would flip if she knew I did this for you. Please don't tell her. I'm not kidding. Hide the basket like under your bed. I'm happy you joined our group. I can't talk to Antonia the way I talk to you. Antonia is my best friend but you actually listen and care about people. I've never had anyone listen to me before. It feels really nice," she said.

"Well, thanks for the basket," I said and smiled.

I turned on the Tellysitter and put on the news while Penny talked.

"Anyway, my clothes look amazing on me. I feel like it will really help me with my eating disorder. You know when a bunch of guys pass you on the street and they don't even look at you because you're not attractive enough but they check out your friend and it makes you feel ugly and worthless?" she said.

"Yeah," I said. "That's called the caveman response. It means nothing," I said.

"Well, that cavedude response will be happening to me! Every guy I pass on the street does a double take and Billy wants me more than ever. I feel like this will help my self-esteem so much!" she said.

'What self-esteem?' I wondered.

"Oh, did you see my wedding announcement?" she asked me.

"No," I said.

Penny gave me her pink electronic pad. She searched on it for Penny and Billy on a website called "Meant to Be" which had dragonflies around the edges and pictures of rocks behind it. Billy held Penny in a staged, loving embrace. Underneath the picture, it read: "Penny, who loves eating goobers and spending time with her wonderful friends, The Dragonflies, and cooking, will marry Billy -- a great man of Braintown."

"Why do you have a pelican and an armadillo on your head in the photo?" I asked.

"Oh, because the pelican and the armadillo mean eternal happiness," Penny said.

"No, it doesn't," I said.

She didn't care.

BREAKING NEWS ON THE TELLYSITTER:
"Gally Bonroe died today at 2:15 BT. Her unexpected death came while filming a cheeseburger commercial for the popular brand "Cool-Girl Burger." Gally was found between two buns. Her final words were "Take a Bite Out of Me," before she was crushed when they accidentally dropped a heavy piece of meat on her. Services will be held tomorrow. King Manu had this to say "Never has a more beautiful thing existed on the earth. She was a part of my most success-ful years. I find comfort in knowing she lived a full life and passed at the old age of 32. Which is pretty old for a woman."

"OMG!" I said.

'Wasn't she our teacher?" Penny asked.

"Yeah," I said.

"Well, anyway... gtg, bitch!" she said.

17

The Perfect Wifey

The following week, I went over to Eivind's house for dinner, as promised. I joined him in his bedroom while we waited for his mom to put the finishing touches on dinner. He started working on his homework and I could see that he was struggling with something because he kept putting his hand on his head and searching through his electronic book for an answer. I sat next to him. "What's wrong?" I asked.

"I can't find the answer to this stupid math problem. One of my buddies said it's in the last pages but I can't find it. I hate trigonometry so much," he said.

I looked at the math problem in the book.

From the top of a 200 meters high building, the angle of depression to the bottom of a second building is 20 degrees. From the same point, the angle of elevation to the top of the second building is 10 degrees. Calculate the height of the second building

"The height of second building = 200 + 200 * tan(10o) / tan(20o)," I said.

"How do you know that?!" he asked.

"Because... tan(200) = 200 / L ....L = 200 / tan(200) and tan(100) = H2 / L ...H2 = L * tan(100) = 200 * tan(100) / tan(200). Therefore the Height of second building is 200 + 200 * tan(100) / tan(200) ... It's so obvious!" I said.

Eivind rushed to the end of the book on his app and found the answer. "That's right!" he said. He got very quiet before asking again, "How did you know that?!"

"Lucky guess!" I said.

"Lucky guess? That's quite a guess," he said. He didn't move but just stared at me like I was a species from another planet. He got up and paced around the room and pulled on his lower lip and then sat on the bed.

'I can't believe I slipped up like that,' I thought. But I was *so* excited to think!

"You're not gonna tell anyone, are you? Please they won't know what to do with me. It's not my fault I know things and I'm smarter than other girls," I said.

Eivind stared at me before making his way back to his seat. "No, I won't say anything," he said. "Do you want to do the rest of my homework for me?" he said, laughing.

"I would love to!" I was so excited to use my brain. I grabbed his electronic book and finished his trig homework, history homework and his English paper. He just lied on his bed and read a comic book until we both heard his mother walking down the hall.

"You're so useful," he said. "I had no idea."

"Dinner is ready!" Eivind's mom said.

"Give me that," he said and took the electronic book I was working with from my hands and put it on his lap and acted like he was reading it.

His mom peeked her head into the room. "Dinner is ready, you two. Come on. Hurry or it's gonna get cold."

"Thanks, mom! Just studying hard. Give me a minute we will be right there."

We made our way to the dining room where I saw a table about three times the size of the one in my home. Eivind told me what to do, "Sit next to my mom," he said.

Dr. Gilbert, Eivind's dad -- who I recognized from the plastic surgery machines -- sat at the head of the table still formally dressed from work, wearing a collar shirt, jacket and tie. Mrs. Gilbert sat by his side, perfectly groomed wearing red lipstick and a red dress. Mrs. Gilbert was in charge at the dinner table and she kept giving me a look that said, "This is how it's done, Alice, and one day you will do it just like this." She lifted her finger, which signaled to the chef and his assistant to bring out the food. As they served everyone, she gave specific orders about how everything should be. "That plate is too ridiculous in size for Dr. Gilbert. No, remove that fork; he needs a larger one. No, my son does not like drinking from large cups.

No, Dr. Gilbert's steak should be well done. Don't give Alice that much food; she is watching her figure."

"I'm not watching my figure," I said.

She smiled and moved her head from side to side signaling her disapproval of my comment.

"So, Alice. I don't believe we have been properly introduced. My name is Samantha Gilbert and this is my husband, Dr. Gilbert," she said.

Dr. Gilbert lifted his left cheek just enough for me to notice the beginning of a smile and continued chewing.

I looked at my plate. What I was served was a piece of lettuce and a thin slice of fish after Samantha told the Chef's Assistant what to serve me.

"I've heard a lot about you, Dr. Gilbert. My mom and dad always talk about what a great doctor you are," I said.

"Really? Then why haven't they come by to see Dr. Gilbert?" he said about himself, not really making eye contact with anyone.

"They tried. But you were all booked up," I said.

"Never mind that. You tell them to call Dr. Gilbert directly and I'm sure Dr. Gilbert can work something out," he said.

I couldn't help but notice all the space between Dr. Gilbert and his wife. They were sitting next to each other but they couldn't seem further apart. Dr. Gilbert's thoughts were off somewhere else. I guess the space between them as a couple didn't surprise me that much since everyone in my town gets married for all the wrong reasons. Like a man pairing up with a woman because she's pretty or a woman wanting a man with status and power. They then sit there bored with each other for the rest of their lives after they find out they have nothing in common.

After my very long pause (that Dr. Gilbert didn't seem to notice) I said, "That would be great! I will let them know."

Dr. Gilbert had already lost interest in me and was playing with his mashed potatoes. "Did you tell them to add salt?" he asked Samantha. "You know I need salt in my food. I like *salt*."

"So you dislike the mashed potatoes?" she asked.

"It's not about whether I like it or not," he said. "I've explained this to you countless times. I need to eat *salt*," he said.

"Do you want me to tell the cook to add more salt?" she asked.

"I don't know," Dr. Gilbert said and kept eating it and like he only made a stink about the lack of salt to have an excuse to be mean to his wife.

I couldn't help but notice what a bad match Samantha and her husband really were the more I stared at them. Dr. Gilbert was fascinated with data, knowledge and how things worked and his wife was incapable of following any train of thought he had. She looked at him like a alien when he said anything at all that could possibly enrich her life. He looked at her with disgust when she talked about shopping and her nails. That must have been lonely for him and her. It was amazing to me they even talked at all! They were complete opposites but they weren't complementary.

"Alice," Eivind whispered to me. "Stop thinking."

"Huh?"

"I can see you thinking a lot. Stop it," he whispered.

I didn't even know you could see someone thinking.

"Honey, did you see my new shoes?" Samantha said smiling and showing off her new pumps.

"Where is the salt, Samantha? I asked for it several times," Dr. Gilbert said.

"Oh, don't be grumpy," Samantha said. "These shoes were a gift. And I just love them! What do you think, honey? Should I wear them with that new black dress you bought me?" she asked.

"I didn't buy you a dress," he said coldly.

"Yeah, you did. Remember? I took your card and I told you I was buying a couple of new dresses," she said.

"Oh... I forgot," he said. "And why were you shopping and not helping Eivind when he needs you most?"

"I was only gone for a few hours. He was in school. I just wanted some time to get away," she said trembling. "To get out of the house. I like going shopping sometimes," She struggled to say and even admit the next part. "It... it... ma-kes me... it makes me... haaa---pppy."

"That time should've been focused on Eivind. I can't believe I have to tell you this," Dr. Gilbert said.

"I'm soooo sorry."' Samantha said. "You're right. I don't know what I was thinking," she said.

"You weren't thinking, obviously," he said.

I could see the mashed potatoes in the center of the table covered in juicy gravy and I looked around as everyone else seemed to be enjoying them. *Why am I being deprived of food like some prisoner?*

"Alice, I'm so glad you were able to join us for dinner tonight. Eivind has never brought a girl home before. He must really like you. You must really be wifey material," Samantha said.

"I guess I am," I said.

"Mom!" Eivind said, embarrassed by the "wifey" mention. Eivind blushed and started eating more and faster. Eivind was already on his third serving of mashed potatoes but the more he ate the happier Samantha was.

"Oh Eivind. Don't be silly. I'm just happy to have Alice here," Samantha said.

"When you find a beautiful girl like Alice, hold on to her," Dr. Gilbert said.

"So, Alice," Samantha said. "How are things at the Institution of Care and Preparation? You know, I went there. It's a great program. King Manu really is great! People will remember his greatness for centuries. I had a ring on my finger six months before the end of my last year. I think I still hold the record as the earliest proposal of the Institution year! But Dr. Gilbert couldn't stay away."

Dr. Gilbert looked annoyed by Samantha.

"Honey, cheer up," Samantha said. "You're so moody."

"Well, I've been working all day. It's stressful," he said to his wife, condescendingly.

Samantha continued, "That Institution doesn't get the credit it deserves. It really transforms the lives of girls. That's why I make Dr. Gilbert write a check every school year to support the facility even though I have no daughter of my own there. Maybe one day I will have a beautiful girl to send there. But until then..." She stopped to chew one small piece of asparagus, which was the only thing I saw her eat. "Anyway, we have big plans for our Eivind. We think he will make a fine member of the King's Court or something else important! A business man too! Look at that face and those eyes!" Samantha said.

"All I need is the right woman by my side," Eivind said while staring at me. "Alice, I have to introduce you to my mentor, Uncle Manu. He's amazing. He's also our King. He changed his name to Manu because he sees himself as the magnificent moon and he designs all his buildings tall enough to try to reach the moon."

I finished my dinner.

"Alice, honey," Samantha said. "Grab your plate and Eivind's and bring it to the kitchen. Eivind sat there talking with his dad while I picked up all his dirty things.

After cleaning up after everyone, Eivind offered to walk me home.

"They're taking out the back. Do you see above the garage? They're pulling all of that out. I would keep it," Eivind said as he walked me home and shared his observations with me about the neighborhood.

"Anyway, maybe sometime soon I can show you how to build model auto-trucks. I keep them in my room," he said.

" I know. That would be great," I said and I meant it.

We made it to my doorstep. Eivind put his tongue in my mouth and his big lips sucked in my small lips in one big suck. I felt like I had no part in the kiss at all and he was just kissing himself. I then felt him suck the air straight out of my body which surprised me at first but then I allowed myself to like it. I didn't know what I was doing. I just followed his sloppy tongue as it went up, down and all over my mouth.

"You're a great kisser," he said.

'I am?' I thought. "Thanks," I said.

"Goodnight, beautiful!" he said as he walked away.

18

Famished

I ran into my house as quickly as possible. My stomach was growling because Samantha barely let me eat a thing.

I ran to the refrigerator in a panic and grabbed a plate of rice and beans and put them on the kitchen table. I took a big spoonful of food and put it in my mouth like I've never eaten anything before a day in my life.

My mother watched from her vacuum cleaner in horror. "What are you doing, Alice? It's after 8BT. You can't eat all that," She jumped off the vacuum cleaner and pulled the plate from my hands.

I pulled it back and we both tugged at the plate at both sides. "I'm so hungry!"

"No, no. Absolutely not. You know you can't have that."

"Please! Give it back, mom!"

"Absolutely not. Go to your room."

"Why won't anyone let me *eeeee-aaaaa-tttttttttt?!* Oh my God... *Leeeeettttt meeeee eeaaaat,"* yelled.

"I'm putting all this food away," my mom said.

I sat on my bed and I felt sharp pains in my stomach and the growls kept me up most of the night. I could actually *feel* my body eating itself and I thought that was really unfair.

At 2BT in the middle of the night, I couldn't take it anymore. I crawled into the kitchen, quietly. I then got up from the floor and tiptoed to the refrigerator and took out a container of lasagna. 'I won't eat all of this. Just some,' I thought.

But I was so hungry I kept eating. Nothing made me feel full. I got up and looked at everything and I panicked. "Fuck! Fuck! *Fuck*!! My mom and dad are gonna kill me!" I washed the containers and took them with me and hid them under my bed before falling asleep.

"ALICE GARCIA, GET IN HERE!!!!!" I heard my mother yell in the morning.

She walked over with an empty pan I forgot to clean. "Did you eat all this?" she asked me in disbelief. "Where are my containers? How can any person eat all this? Did you do this, Alice Garcia?"

"Guilty," I said.

"How does a human eat all this food in one sitting?" she asked me again.

"I was really hungry," I said. "No one lets me eat!"

"You eat too much for a girl! I've been saying this to you your entire life. Girls eat like birds. Not like huge bears! And you have to wax your eyebrows. They're too hairy!"

She was angry and the more she thought about my bold move to actually eat, the angrier she got. I could hear her outside of my room talking to herself, opening and closing kitchen cabinets and then scrubbing the floors harder than usual. Finally, she did what she always does when she doesn't know how to handle or deal with her own emotions in a healthy and positive way. She pulled out the TurboBlaster again and hit "Maximum Vacuuming," which not only turns on the vacuum cleaner full blast to suck in the toughest dirt, but also destroys the fibers of the carpet which drives my dad nuts. The sound resembles that of nails on a chalkboard. But it also signaled to me she meant business. I had to do something. She was solely responsible for the message that would reach my father about me.

"Mom!" I yelled, while she spun around and round on top of the machine. "Mom!" I said louder. "A rich boy is interested in me...Dr. Gilbert's son is interested in me."

My mom immediately turned off the TurboBlaster. "Dr. Gilbert... *the* Dr. Gilbert... the most respected doctor in town... *that* Dr. Gilbert?"

"Yeah," I said. "I had dinner with Eivind and the whole family yesterday."

"Oh, my God. Oh, my God," she said. "I have to wake up your father and tell him. Jorge, Jorge, wake up!" she yelled.

My dad came out of his room. "What's with all the noise out here, Tazia?"

"Jorge, our daughter is going to marry into the Gilbert family!"

"I didn't say that," I said. "We just had dinner, dad."

"Don't listen to her. She doesn't understand this stuff. That's exactly what is going to happen," my mom said.

My father smiled but even when he smiles he always looks like he's in so much pain he wants to just leave it all and move to another dimension. He never would. In his own way, he really does love me and my mom. "Dr. Gilbert is a very respected man," he said after his shoulders relaxed and he let out a breath showing relief that someone would marry me. Then he walked to the kitchen and noticed the sink was full of dirty cups. "Who is going to wash all this? Who left these cups here?" my dad asked.

'Oh, Alice will get to them now," my mom said.

"I didn't dirty those cups," I said.

"Take care of this," my dad said to my mother before preparing to head back to his room. "Let's not change the order of how we do things in this house."

LAURA ELIZABETH HERNANDEZ

"Yes, dad. You know, when mom passes away and I'm married, you should get a maid to replace both of us," I said.

"I know you're right, Alice. I'll have to find a good one too. Someone with the best domestic abilities of both of you. Replacing both of you won't be easy," he said.

"Dad, I was kidding," I said.

"What's there to kid about? I'm going to need someone to do all this stuff. Who would do it when you're both gone?"

"Maybe you..."

"Alice, I have to say you have one the wildest and best senses of humor I have ever seen," my dad said.

19

The Question

Later that night, I went back to Eivind's house. My routine was pretty much the same with Eivind. I would do all his homework, tutor him a bit, then he would read some comic electronic books, then we would make out. Today he got an erection and ejaculated in his pants before falling asleep. It struck me, while Eivind was sleeping, that I had to tutor Eivind about everything. He was slow to learn things and I had to repeat everything over and over again. The fact that Eivind was a passive idiot worked for me and my long-term goals. After taking a short nap with Eivind, his mom knocked on the door.

"Oh, how cute. You two are taking a nap together. Why don't you two join us in the living room?" Samantha asked politely. She was afraid Eivind and I would get busy in there if she didn't pull us out of bed.

"Come on, lovebirds," Samantha said.

I got to the living room and found Dr. Gilbert on the couch watching the Tellysitter and Samantha sat directly in front of me on her stiff, white couch.

"Son," Dr. Gilbert said. "King Manu is excited about all the great things he's hearing about your performance in school. I'm happy that your grades have improved the way that they have. If you keep this up you'll join his Council of Twelve Men. There's a slot opening next year," Dr. Gilbert said.

"I know, dad," Eivind said. "I've been working really hard."

No, he hasn't. *I've* been working really hard.

"King Manu is an incredible man. It would be a *dream* to work so close to him," Eivind said.

"What do you think about his new economic plan?" Dr. Gilbert asked his son.

"Well," he said as he made some weird movement with his mouth, the kind you make when something tastes bad. "I don't really want to get into all that right now. You know. A heated debate and all," Eivind said.

'Liar,' I thought. He doesn't know.

Dr. Gilbert shrugged it off and kept watching the Tellysitter.

I wanted to earn some points and save them for later in case I needed a favor from Eivind. So I said, "Dr. Gilbert, Eivind hates talking about politics and economics at home. He was going on and on today about how he feels those plans will do nothing to fix the growing income inequality."

"Well, I disagree with you, son. King Manu is right on. Why do you care about income inequality? You should care about a growing economy. But you're still young. You'll see once you enter the real world. You sound like a goddamn radical, son. And Alice you sound like those tales of those crazy Shelatza women. Let my son speak for himself."

"Shelatza women?" I asked, pretending not to know anything about them.

"They are women you need to know nothing about. It doesn't concern you," Dr. Gilbert said.

Eivind whispered to me "Those are very bad women, ok? Just change the subject."

"What did they do?" I asked.

"Just bad things they weren't supposed to do, now drop it," Eivind said.

Samantha grabbed my hand and had me follow her into her closet. Her closet was the size of a bedroom. She had over six hundred pairs of shoes in every color along a very brightly lit wall. She also had every sweater in every color imaginable and every pricey fabric ever made. She started searching through her cashmere section and picked several sweaters in different colors. "Red, green, blue, white," she grabbed them all.

"I want you to have these," she said.

"Oh, no, please. It's really not necessary," I said.

"You're too modest. I want you to have them. Feel the fabric." She put it up against my face and rubbed it all over my hands and face. "See how soft that is? The girls at the Institution will be so envious. Especially the ones that know a thing or two about cashmere... and those are the girls you want to impress anyway. And here's a little tip to cover up that scar. Press Q4 Foundation neutral rosy J17."

"Thank you, Samantha. That's very sweet," I said.

I feel so sorry for Samantha. She seems so lonely in her closet staring at her shoes. I hugged her and she refused to let me go. "I have to get back to Eivind," I said.

"Of course," she said.

As I walked out of her room, Eivind grabbed my hand and escorted me outside. "Alice," he said. "Everything is coming together perfectly And it's all because of you."

"What are you talking about?" I asked.

"You know... I'll have a great job in the future and a beautiful wife by my side. What everyone wants. Great job. Beautiful wife. Wealth. The right friends!" he said.

"That's your dream?" I asked him.

"That's everyone's dream. What's wrong with that?"

"Nothing, I guess."

"All the guys will see you with me and they'll think: 'Wow, he has such a beautiful wife. Which is why, Alice, I'd like to ask you...will you be my wife? I feel like we could make a good team," he said.

I thought about Eivind and how he was harmless compared to the other boys in my town and I said, "Yes. Yes, I'll marry you."

Eivind smiled and placed a wedding ring on my finger. It felt heavy and weighed my hand down. We shared a kiss.

20

"Never Take That Off"

When I got to the Mirror Room the next morning, the Dragonflies RUSHED to my side and insisted on one thing: *seeing the diamond.*

"Holy cow... look at that thing!" Penny said. "It's worth more than your life. I'm so jelly. It's a Rampurk!"

Mrs. Jackson walked over to where I was standing and said, "Let me look at the diamond."

She held my hands in hers and I watched as tears rolled down her face. "Should I take it off for the Mirror exercise?" I asked.

"Take it off? Oh, honey, you *never* have to take that off!" she said, before she hugged me. "And, you can supervise going forward. I'm so proud of you," she said. She took my hand, stretched it out in the air in front of all the girls and said, *"yes!"*

It was stupid.

"I knew she wasn't *that* pretty but she was pretty enough to marry rich. That's why I was like, I'll be friends with this girl or whatever," Antonia said.

"That's why you decided to be my friend?" I asked her.

"Yeah," she said, raising her eyebrow.

That's such a weird thing to think and even weirder thing to say out loud. That I'm her friend because she saw the potential for riches in me and she found me somewhat attractive. How bizarre. But the Dragonflies aren't my friends. Friends only exist on shows on the Tellysitter.

My duty as supervisor basically meant I stood there calling names with a clipboard in my hand. New students were walking into the Mirror Room now and some unwed girls were also there.

"He's been ignoring me," Penny said.

"Who?" I asked.

"Billy... At first he was so excited about my surgery and calling me every single day but now he's distant," she said.

"But I thought he liked *gigantic* tits," I said.

"He does," she said, looking confused.

Penny's eyes are looking creepy these days. They have this frozen, cold look about them and she's barely talking since she's in so much pain.

"I dunno," Penny told me while she stood next to me waiting for her turn. "Billy told me I have ugly toes and he hates my hair."

"What a nice thing to say!" I said.

"Here, hold my stuff. I'm heading to Mirror 1, bee-atch," she said.

Penny was taking this class more seriously than ever these days. She *really* ripped herself apart in the mirror.

She began, "I have ugly lips, lizardly skin, crooked legs, a limp, UGLY toes, a waist that is built for an elephant, my tits are deformities and my hair is dry," she said.

"Are you alright?" I asked her. "That's a bit much for Mirror 1, Penny. Maybe she should take a breather, Mrs. Jackson?"

Penny looked demonic by the time she made her way to the 3rd and final mirror. Her reflection was completely distorted from where I was standing. "I am the ugliest woman to ever walk this earth, my pores, they're not even pores, they're huge HOLES, and everyone can see them. My body is just *holes*. My arms are long and they remind me of a grasshopper. My breasts look like infected balloons and they pull my back forward to reveal the monstrous hunchback that I am and will always be. I hate you! I hate you! I hate you!" She fell to the floor in tears.

"Okay. Why don't we take a break, yes?" Mrs. Jackson said. "But good work, Penny."

I went to where Penny was on the floor and I patted her back and removed the hair from her face. "Penny, I'm worried about you," I said.

"Don't be," she said as she got up from the floor and stormed out of the class.

Mrs. Jackson approached me and asked me to take a turn. "Alice, do you want to give the other girls some time to cool down? Maybe do it for old time's sake and show them how it's done?"

"Sure," I said. "No problem."

Mirror 1 was immediately playing its usual mind games on me. It made my head slightly larger and my acne look worse. But I could see the distortion so clearly now. "You know what, Mrs. Jackson. I think I'm just gonna go straight to Mirror 3. What do you think?"

"It's up to you. I mean, the mirrors are designed that way so that you can gradually take it all in but if you feel like you can go straight to Mirror 3, please do. Show these girls how it's done," she said.

I placed myself between the cubes in Mirror 3. My legs were already expanding in size, my acne took over my entire body, my waist tripled, my hair was so thin I appeared bald in the mirror. All the girls in the class circled around me waiting for me to reveal it all.

I closed my eyes and thought about the beautiful Shelatza pink sky. I could see it so clearly and it made me feel strong and beautiful. "I have beautiful hair, my eyes are big, hazel, and cute. My legs are toned and in incredible shape. My thighs are thick at the top but strong. My skin is soft and I'm still very young and beautiful. And I have the cutest nose ever!" I said. "Nothing is wrong with me. Nothing at all, Mrs. Jackson."

"Look again, Alice," Mrs. Jackson said. "You're clearly not seeing what's in the mirror."

I looked again and the distortions were so ridiculous and over the top I let out a chuckle. "Nothing is wrong with me at all. I'm a hottie marrying a rich dude. I'm really cute!" I said.

I started walking out the door and Mrs. Jackson started walking quickly to catch up with me.

"Alice, I expect you to still participate in this class," she said.

"I *am* participating in this class. I just did. As Supervisor and as a student."

"But you didn't do what you were supposed to."

"I don't have to. I have my ring. And I got the man. So based on what you've told us this entire time, I really don't need to come to this class anymore. I'm above it. And if you have a problem with that why don't you take it up with Dr. Gilbert and his wife. Nothing would give me greater pleasure than telling them you are forcing me to work in a class I don't even need anymore. It's kind of insulting to them, isn't it? I mean, are you still trying to get me a better proposal?"

"No!"

"Then I think I don't need this class anymore."

"Fine," she said. "But I will be reporting this behavior to Mrs. Ruthberry."

21

Showtime

That night, I couldn't sleep. I was having a dream about Ayoka, Asais, Jujuki and the other Shelatza women burning and I woke up shaking. 'I have to destroy all of the machines in this town *now*,' I thought. 'I can't let my friends down.'

At 2 am BT, I broke into the Institution. I got in the Romantic Booth and stared at DJ Wally's annoying face. "I know you ladies are looking for love," he said. "And while you do, here's is some music to hang on to that lovin' feeling. Yeah! Love is a wonderful thang, baby."

A music video started playing featuring a man and a bunch of voluptuous girls shaking their butts in front of him.

Song: Panties in the Dryer
"Your panties are in my dryer, bitch
Clean them with my boxers, now
Scrub the floors, bitch
Serve me dinner"

'WTF?' I thought. Is that even music?

I hate this booth! I started typing in the code from memory to destroy the romantic booth.

@Romantic FANTASY- **BOYCRAZY**- 4title R.I. Pstartstart +**BOYCRAZY**+ FANTASY desktopcopy%romaticreg VIRUS DETECTED + FANTASY + FANTASY MAN_ **UNREALISTIC EXPECTATIONS** _ batscopy Wire + R+ Booth. PSHUTDOWN + RSHUTDOWN + RSHUTDOWN +%% calctskill + iexplore+ **MYSOGYNISTIC LYRICS**
    "ERROR ERROR ERROR"

Damn it! That's not it. What is it again? What's the rest of the code?!

Wait... is it? + R SHUTDOWN +R SHUTDOWN +
Shit!!! Let me try this...
/ @ROmantic + HEAT + RTERMINATION//

I started to smell smoke and I could see smoke coming from beneath my seat. The door was locked and the smoke was starting to grow around me. "What the hell?"

DJ Wally's face broke into small rectangles, that turned to straight lines and DJ Wally appeared randomly saying, "Anything? Love? Yeah? Loving! Longing! You got unrealistic! Yeah! Expectations!" Then I watched DJ Wally's head melt on the screen completely. The bars on the side of the chair wrapped around me and held me in place. I tried to remove them but they had a tight grip on me. I couldn't believe it: the machine was trying to eat me alive! I pictured myself as someone who had superhuman strength; then pictured myself escaping the machine. I lifted the bars off me and freed myself from the machine.

I ran out of the school and hid behind a tree as I watched police auto-trucks and fire auto-trucks pull up at the Institution. I found the shortest path to my house, climbed through my bedroom window, put my clothes in a garbage bag under my bed and fell asleep at 4:05 BT.

Early the next morning, I heard the Tele-k-phone ring.

"Hello," I said.

"Alice, wake up bitch," Antonia said on the other end. "Huge fucking fire at school," she said.

"Is everyone okay?" I asked.

Who cares?" she said. "Turn on the Tellysitter. I think King Manu is talking about it."

I got up and looked at the Tellysitter.

"WHAT WILL GIRLS THINK ABOUT NOW? THESE BOOTHS GAVE THEM SOMETHING TO STIMULATE THEIR MINDS. A FOCUS. A PURPOSE. IF GIRLS ARE NOT THINKING ABOUT BOYS ALL THE TIME IT HURTS ALL OF US AS A SOCIETY. WE KNOW

WHAT HAPPENS WHEN GIRLS THINK. THEY HAVE THESE SILLY, INSIGNIFICANT IDEAS THAT EXHAUST US AND SERVE NO PURPOSE. I WANT TO ASSURE EVERYONE THAT WE WILL REPLACE THE MACHINE. YOU HAVE MY WORD," he said.

It was Saturday and my parents were at a friend's house. I didn't have any plans and was under so much stress, I knocked out. I spent the rest of the day in bed.

22

Alibi

I jumped out of my bedroom window at 02:05 BT. I walked through the woods by myself to avoid being seen on the street and dressed all in black. When I got to the Institution I was relieved to find that the window leading up to the Mirror Room was open. I climbed through the window and stood in the classroom in front of the mirrors.

I stared at my reflection in Mirror 3 and watched as my arms grew long, scaly, and green. I watched my head grow in size as I walked closer and closer to my own reflection. I decided to ignore my reflection, which was really easy to do these days and pulled out a keypad connected to the mirror and began typing the code.

@Mirror + SELF + HARDEST _ON_SELF- *no inner beauty* M SHUTDOWN. WIRE. CALCIEXPLORE-BEAUTY SKIN DEEP_ **UNREALISTIC STANDARD OF BEAUTY**- M SHUTDOWN- Monster Reflection----*TOO THIN<* M SHUTDOWN--M *TOO FAT*----M ROOM THIGHS TOUCH- M ROOM- HAIR TOO THIN- BUTT TOO LARGE--M I EPLORE SHUTDOWN-DESKTOP-

FEET TOO BIG -- EYES TOO SMALL - INSUFFICIENT EYEBROWS - -SHUTDOWN- NOT ENOUGH. *TOES TOO LARGE* -- NAILS TOO THIN --- INSUFFICIENT- INSUFFICIENT— INSUFFICIENT- INSUFFICIENT- *NOSE TOO LARGE-* EARS TOO POINTY- INSUFFICIENT = INSUFFICIENT- HATE SELF- **HATE REFLECTION**- EAT LESS- *DISTORT IMAGE*- DISTORT IMAGE- DISTORT IMAGE - FUNHOUSE- FUNHOUSE- SHUTDOWN -MSHUTDOWN-DESKTOP

The mirrors started cracking and I started to smell the scent of fire growing.

Mirror 1 cracked! Then Mirror 2: "BOOM!" And finally Mirror 3: "BOOM!" Part of the glass from the 3rd mirror flew in my direction and almost cut my arm.

I heard someone coming to the room. It was General XY♂ Harry. "Who are you?! What the hell are you doing on private property? What did you do to those mirrors?" he asked.

He grabbed my hair and ripped off a chunk of it as I ran and hid.

The classroom was filling up with smoke and I couldn't see him anymore and he couldn't see me either. I was able to run out of the room.

But he knows the color of my hair and how tall I am. I need an alibi. I immediately thought of Eivind. I ran to his house and knocked on his window.

"Psst. Ei-vind. Psst," I said, quietly.

"What are you doing here?" he asked, as he rubbed his right eye before opening the window.

"I missed you. I wanted to see you. Isn't that romantic?" I said.

"Yeah. But Alice, it's really late. Can't this wait until tomorrow?"

"I'm being spontaneous," I said.

Eivind grabbed my arm and helped me through the window and he made a place for me next to him on his bed after removing some pillows of his favorite superhero, "The Groubster Man."

"You have to leave before my parents wake up," he said.

"No problem. I will."

23

Choices

I went to the Institution the next day and I saw Antonia outside.

"You look a little tired. Is something wrong? Working late or something?" Antonia asked me.

"I'm not feeling well," I said.

I noticed two police auto-trucks in front of our school and several General XY♂ officers walking with General XY♂ Harry. We were all escorted to the Mirror Room. The room was filthy and dark and it was difficult to breathe in there.

General XY♂ Harry made his way across the room and looked at each of us. He asked one girl to step forward and then another one as he passed me. I let out a sigh of relief but before I got the chance to catch my breath he turned back around and held my hair in his hand and felt it with his fingertips.

"You're Alice, right?"

"Yes," I said.

"Alice..." General XY♂ Harry said. "Everyone but Alice can leave."

The girls rushed out of the room and Antonia and Penny looked at me with concern before walking out, too. "WTF is going on?" Antonia asked Penny. "Why are they keeping Alice? Do you think they're arresting her because she looks like shit today?" Antonia asked.

"Could be. She looks horrible," Penny said.

"Something really bad happened here last night, Alice," General XY Harry told me. "There was criminal activity as you can see by the current state of what was once a happy and safe place for the girls at this Institution. But you wouldn't believe it if I told you... A girl caused all of this destruction. Crazy, right?"

"Sir, that's horrible. A girl?"

"Yup. And I think that girl was you... What do you think about that?"

"I don't think, Sir. This fine Institution teaches us not to do that. I don't know why you would think that I could think, Sir," I said.

"You're not a citizen," he said. "But I have to arrest you."

I was handcuffed and placed in General XY Harry's auto-truck and taken to a prison a few blocks from my house. When I got there they threw me in a cell and shut the door.

I heard two men talk about the damage I had done and how it would cost over 20,000 dollars to fix the classroom and another 50,000 dollars to reinstall the mirrors.

"You're gonna pay big time for what you did, Alice," General XY Harry said. "I know you destroyed the Romantic Booth, too. I just know it," he said.

"Sir, I'm just a girl," I said. "Do you really think I'm capable of this?"

He grabbed my arm tightly. "Please let go of my arm," I said. "This is all a terrible misunderstanding. And my fiancé will see that I'm released!" I said.

"We'll see about that," he said.

Hours later, Eivind finally walked in with his parents.

"Eivind!" I yelled.

"Alice should not be here," Eivind said sternly. "She was with me last night at my house. So she couldn't have done anything."

"At what time did Alice come to your house last night?" General Harry XY♂ asked.

"At 10 BT, sir. And she didn't leave until first thing in the morning," Eivind said.

"Do I have your word?" he asked Eivind.

"Yes, sir. You do. Now please let my beautiful fiancé go."

"This is insane," General XY Harry said. "I know it's her."

"Remove my future daughter-in-law's handcuffs at once," Dr. Gilbert said and Harry did as ordered.

Eivind kissed me on the cheek and held me in his arms. "You're okay, now" he said.

"My poor little Alice," Samantha Gilbert said as she patted my head in the auto-truck on the way to their house. "I'm angry that you stayed over but I can't believe they put you in that cell. My goodness! What you must've gone through. Look at your hair and your nails. You're a mess, sweetheart," she said.

I went to Eivind's house but his parents didn't allow us to go to his room. It was now officially off limits.

"No time alone in Eivind's bedroom. Understood?" Samantha said to Eivind and me.

"Understood," we both said.

Dr. Gilbert chimed in. "I still can't believe the nerve of General Harry XY♂. Treating our girl in such a manner. I'm gonna go to my study and write a letter to their department head," he said.

Eivind and I were served a warm meal. Eivind was sitting at the other end of the table and he wasn't speaking much.

"What?" I said as I chewed on mashed potatoes, surprised they were letting me eat.

"Nothing," he said.

"What, Eivind? Why the hell are you sitting so far away from me? How am I supposed to talk to you like this?" I said.

Eivind reluctantly grabbed his plate and sat right next to me. "Alice," he whispered. "I don't know what the hell you're doing. But you have to promise me you'll stop before you ruin both of our lives."

"I'm doing what I have to do, Eivind. The Romantic Booth, The Mirror Room. Those things were evil. They were hurting girls."

"But that's not your problem anymore. You're almost out of there. We're gonna get married soon and I'll protect you. There are lots of things in this town that are unfair Alice. If I went around town destroying everything that upset me I would be in serious trouble. You just can't do that!"

I didn't say anything but everything Eivind said really got to me. If he only knew about Shelatza and the girls and what I know. But I couldn't tell him that. He would think I'm crazy.

"Thank you for what you did for me today," I said. "You saved my life."

"You're my fiancé now. I can't separate myself from what you do," he said.

A few hours later, as I grabbed my coat to leave Eivind's house, Eivind stopped me. "Alice, promise me you'll stop this. Okay? For both our sakes? For my future."

I nodded and took off.

Eivind is right. I have to stop. I can't keep doing this. This isn't at all who I am. I'm destroying private property in the middle of the night and getting locked in jail. If it wasn't for Eivind today I would be in a world of trouble. But can I really leave those women in Sheltaza? Can I live my life and forget what I know about the machines in Braintown?

24

"I Do"

I was marrying Eivind to keep up appearances. I was wearing a white dress that made me itch and it was fluffy and uncomfortable. Samantha picked it out.

And since I didn't really care what I wore, I just put it on. I didn't eat today to fit in this thing, so of course, I'm starving. My dress had a slit on the right side which showed most of my thigh and lace in the back. I couldn't wait to take it off.

"You look like an anorexic model. Love it!" Penny said.

"Thanks?" I said.

"You look so pale and bony. I love it!" Antonia said.

"Pale is so in right now. Sickly is the new healthy. I'm so excited about your speed wedding. Getting married in under ten minutes is so cool," she said.

My mother came to see me for some alone time before my father, Jorge, came to pick me up to walk me down the aisle. "Honey, you look like a princess. I'm so proud of you," she said.

'For what?' I thought. I haven't done anything.

"I hope you don't mind but I gave a quote to the press on your behalf about the wedding," my mom said.

I grabbed my electronic pad and looked up the article and found my quote written by my mother as me. "Today is such a special day. We took so much time and so much detail to prepare for this special day to marry the love of my life, Eivind Gilbert. This will be the happiest day of my life and I know I will feel like a Princess."

"Mom, why did you add that Princess part? You know I hate stuff like that."

"Well, you *are* a Princess," she said.

"No, I'm not a Princess," I said.

"Are you ready, Alice?" my father asked, waiting for me to finish up my discussion with my mother.

I wanted my mother to look at me. I wanted my mother to really see me. Especially right now when I felt more invisible than ever in this stupid, ridiculous dress.

"Mom... Mom," I said. " I'm good at math and other things, too," I said.

"You look absolutely stunning," she said. "But, honey, suck in your stomach."

"Mom, stop picking at me. Did you hear me? I'm really smart."

"SUCK. IN. YOUR. STOMACH," she said.

I can't believe I still love this woman.

"Sure, Mom," I said, sucking in my stomach.

I joined my father and he began walking me down the aisle.

"Today is a very special day. Do you Eivind Gilbert, take Alice Marcia..."

"Garcia, not Marcia," I said.

"Oh... I read that wrong. Sorry. Do you take Alice Garcia to be your lovely wedded wife to love and to hold in sickness and in health as long as you both shall live?"

"I do," he said without hesitation.

"And do you, Alice Garcia, take Eivind of the Gilbert family to love and to hold in sickness and in health as long as you both shall live?"

"I...do," I said with hesitation, because I don't respect Eivind.

"My daughter is Mrs. Gilbert!" I heard my mom yell to the heavens followed by applause.

"They are the hottest and richest couple ever!" Antonia yelled.

"And they'll have hot babies, too!" Penny said.

I threw my bouquet to a bunch of eager women behind me including the Dragonflies. I turned around to find out Antonia caught it.

"That means I'm next, bitch!" she said.

Dr. Gilbert got up and behaved in a way I've never seen him behave before. Like a totally decent human being! He treated Samantha very differently with his public mask on than he did at the dinner table.

"This cake," he began as he smiled. "This wedding cake wouldn't be what it is without my wife Samantha's warmth."

Everyone awed and ooed.

He said again, liking the attention, but louder this time, "If there is any warmth at all in this cake it's because of my beautiful wife, Samantha!"

Samantha got up and he put his arm around her in a very rehearsed way and smiled. "Today I dedicate the marriage of Alice and Eivind to my Samantha. This is for you, honey."

Then they kissed.

"Awwwww," everyone swooned.

Immediately after getting married everyone started watching my stomach for any signs of a baby bump.

"So are you?" Antonia asked.

"Am I what?" I asked.

"You know... *pregnant?*" Antonia asked me.

"Antonia, how can I be pregnant? I just got married right this second," I said.

"Oh, my bad. I guess you're right. But soon, right?'

"She'll have a baby very soon," my mom said. "All women want babies."

"I don't," I said.

"Yes, you do," my mom said.

"No, I don't."

"Yes, you do."

"No. I *don't.*"

"YES. YOU. DO," my mom said. "Bye, sweetheart."

25

Honeymoon Period

After the ceremony, Eivind and I went to our new home, which was right next door to Dr. Gilbert's house. The house was breathtaking. It was all white at the end of a *cul de sac* and it had a beautiful, new auto-truck parked in front of the garage with a bow on it for Eivind. It was the biggest home on the block and it had huge windows on the first floor. Big enough so that everyone could look into our home and see how rich we were, because that's all that matters to anyone.

I walked in with our bags and my jaw dropped when I saw that I had not one living room but two. And a dining room that was four times bigger than my bedroom.

A woman came and took the bags from my hand. "I will be the caretaker of the house. Food will be ready at 6:00 BT," she said.

'Good. At least I don't have to cook today,' I thought.

Eivind and I ate dinner while he read the news on the UCNCFM. Eivind wasn't feeling well so we just went to bed.

"Eivind..." I said in bed. "Are you awake? "

I jumped on top of him and tried to seduce my new husband. "Are you feeling hot, baby? Do you want me, baby?" I said as I grabbed onto my breasts.

Eivind freaked out. He threw me off his bed.

"What are you doing?!"

"Um... trying to hook up with my husband. I'm horny."

"You're acting like a whore!"

"Eivind, how can I be a whore when I'm trying to hook up with my own husband?"

"Don't be a slut!" he said and slapped me across the face.

"Why can't you just know your place?" he added and then turned over and turned off the light. I couldn't move and couldn't think of anything to say. Later that night as I lay in bed, I couldn't stop thinking about Ayoka, Jujuki, Asais, Check and the Pink Dragon. I walked back and forth alone in my beautiful living room and lit a cigarette. I grabbed a leather jacket and headed outside. I wasn't sure where I was going. I walked to the Institution but it was as if my body took me there without consulting with my brain. I could see General XY Harry guarding the school. There were also several General XY officers blocking the side entrance.

I went to the basement of the Institution and stood in front of the window. I opened the window, climbed through and slowly headed to the Prince Charming class. The room was extremely dark and I kept the lights off. I made my way to the monitor and pulled out the keyboard and turned it on. As soon as I did Penny's Prince Charming Billy appeared on the screen.

"Hello, Penny," he said.

"I'm not Penny, you idiot," I said.

"How can I make your life better?" he said.

"Interesting question. You could've made Penny's life better by liking her just as she is, you degenerate," I said.

"Excuse me?" He said.

I looked at the side of the monitor and it measured that my attitude was off the charts.

"Penny... I..." he said.

"Shut up," I said. "Stop talking."

I started typing.

@Hero+*Thinking for You*_SAVE ME! SAVE ME! SAVE ME! Cinderella + Eric+ No Voice_____*The Little Mermaid* -++++ Desktop +++++ Cool Girl &&&&&& PRINCEM**SHUTDOWN**....THE BEAST _____*Aladdin can show you whole new world*++++DESKTOP ----- **ROBIN HOOD** SAVE ME! Desktop **SHUTDOWN**.

I watched as Billy's head turned into a bunch of scattered dots on the screen. Then he said, "Baby... Great House... Attitude... Hero... Hero + Thinking for you. Save, Save, SHUTDOWN."

The printer started printing the word ATTITUDE over again and again and the papers started to fill up in the class.

I heard a noise. I hid underneath one of the desks. "What's going on?" I heard General Harry XY ask another officer.

General Harry XY stormed into the class and looked around. I held on to my leg to keep it from shaking and held my breath. "There's no one in here," he said as he closed the door.

I waited until he was gone from the area before running out of the room and heading to the auditorium that houses the plastic surgery machines. I had to move fast.

I saw one machine alone in the corner. It still had bloodstains all over it. I looked around for the pad that Dr. Gilbert usually types on when each girl goes into the machines. I know that the pad connects and runs all of the machines. I saw a small board coming out of machine #2 and I walked over to it. When I pulled out the keypad the screen turned on. On the screen, I saw Jade's old picture and her selections: a larger ass, legs the size of arms and a smaller waist among other things. It was disgusting. There was no "after" picture of Jade. Just an empty space with an X over it.

I typed in the code Asais gave me to destroy the machines. Seconds later, smoke started coming out of all three machines. One machine started spinning quickly and smashed into a wall. I saw images of all the girls that went through the machines on my monitor, followed by just their parts: My old breasts, my new breasts, Penny's breasts. But the screen also began to burn.

I started coughing and the smoke was making it difficult for me to breathe. The alarm started ringing and my hands started shaking and I could barely see anything until someone entered through the main door with a torch motor lamp and focused his light right on me.

"I knew it! Alice Gilbert!" General XY Harry said. He pulled a Talk-e Phone from his back pocket. "I'm here at the Institution of Care and Preparation. We have a break-in. Need back up immediately. Send fire auto-trucks. Sprinklers have been activated. I have a girl in custody."

I typed a code into the board for the last remaining machine that was still intact.

CODE; slide block, head north MACHINE WHITE NUMBER THREE
Pounds of Force = 50,000 pounds
Cylinder Rod End Area = 21.19 square inches

Pounds of Force Needed ÷ Cylinder Area = 50,000 ÷ 21.19 = 2,359.60 PSI

I hit "enter." I watched the machine slide and block General XY Harry and the other officers.

"Everyone is gonna know what you did, Alice. I'll tell everyone! I swear to God I'll tell everyone what I saw here today!" he yelled as I ran away in the other direction.

I headed out of the school and I tried not to think about how much trouble I'm in.

'How could I explain myself this time? What was I *thinking?* They saw me,' I thought.

I got a very sick feeling in my stomach and a tingling in my fingertips before I started throwing up by a tree. I sat on the ground by the tree and stared at my trembling hands, then closed my eyes and thought of the pink Shelatza sky. It did calm me down.

I spent the next two days alone in the woods. Part of me was hiding and the other part of me just needed time to gather my thoughts.

I was finally calm enough to pull a UCNCFM electronic pad from my pocket to see if any news had been reported about my break in.

I typed in "BRAINTOWN HEADLINES" and a bunch of stories popped up:

"MENTALLY DISTURBED GIRL DESTROYS PRIVATE PROPERTY

RICH AND PRETTY FUGITVE ON THE LOOSE

RICH AND CRAZY? WHO IS ALICE GILBERT?

GILBERT FAMILY SHAMED

PERSONAL ESSAY: ALICE'S MOTHER SHARES HEARTFELT LETTER TO DAUGHTER ABOUT NOT TREATING HER MENTAL ILLNESS SOONER

TOWN IN SHOCK OVER UNGRATEFUL GIRL'S BEHAVIOR: "WHO DOES SHE THINK SHE IS?"

SAMANTHA GILBERT: "STOP CALLING HER MRS. GILBERT! SHE IS NO DAUGHTER OF MINE!"

DR. GILBERT WRITES CHECK FOR $25,000 DOLLARS TO REPLACE PLASTIC SURGERY MACHINE

DR. GILBERT WRITES CHECK FOR $50,000 TO TREAT MENTAL ILLNESS IN THE COMMUNITY

I searched for the location of the final machine: "Brain location Machine stored? Where does brain and glass ceiling live."

INCORRECT QUESTION INCORRECT QUESTION INCORRECT QUESTION.

"CENTER BRAIN. storage. patriarchy center. Where can I find the ceiling of glass and the brain"

King Manu Bachelor Pad
12 Meaningless Road
Basement.

I had only one thought going through my complicated and lively brain while I stared at the sky in the woods:

Destroying the Brain. The brain that keeps all the girls in Braintown imprisoned. The Brain that has limited our options and forced us to see ourselves as nothing but amusement, eye candy, sexual playthings, workers, housekeepers, well behaved girls and cheerleaders for men. The Brain that silenced me and made me fear talking and thinking. The Brain that hurt Shelatza women and stole their chance at a life. The Brain that made all of us value beauty over intelligence or substance. I hated it more than all the other machines in this town and nothing gives me greater joy than the thought of destroying it.

26

Manu

I arrived at King Manu's bachelor pad. I saw empty bottles, a huge Tellysitter and a king-sized bed. I also saw pictures of King Manu's conquests, including Gally Bonroe.

I made my way to the basement and found the Brain. It was lit and bright. It had images of "perfect" women along the sides (and codes). I pulled out the board and began typing the code to destroy the brain. On the left of the screen, I saw my reflection and above it, it said "The Mirror Room." I looked at my reflection and I had scaly green skin again. My thighs were big and rubbing together, my eyebrows were hairy, my nose pointy. Another screen came down and I saw DJ Wally. *"I KNOW YOU'RE LOOKING FOR LOVE."* The music started playing full blast, *"How do I Live without you? Baby without you I'm nothing."* Then, another screen:"Hi, Alice. I'm Eivind, your Prince Charming. I'll be your hero."

The music was blasting in my ears. I had to cover them with both hands. My reflection made me uncomfortable but I went back to the keyboard and began typing the final code:

--BRAIN-GIRL-CONTROL-BRAIN-LIMITS

DESKTOP # VIRUS # DESTROY _UNLOCK

ALL THAT MATTERS ARE A WOMAN'S LOOKS--

Woman is a misbegotten man and has a faulty and defective nature in comparison to his. Therefore she is unsure in herself. What she cannot get, she seeks to obtain through lying and diabolical deceptions. And so, to put it briefly, one must be on one's guard with every woman, as if she were a poisonous snake and the horned devil.

...The word and works of God is quite clear, that women were made either to be wives or prostitutes. *–Martin Luther* #PROTESTANT REFORMERS SEXISM.

SERVE OTHERS- BOY CRAZY---- BOY CRAZY---

*PUT SELF LAST*____ %%%% VIRUS ____

DESKTOP ____ DESKTOP _____VIRUS//////

3:12 PRESS Misogyny *Marie Antoinette Let them Eat Cake* ++HATED QUEEN_++GIVE US AN HEIR—

has been said in the past—

Women ARE DEFORMITIES_ARISTOTLE --

----FREUD#### PENIS ENVY ---SUBSERVIENT-

---NEVER PRETTY ENOUGH %%%%% THIGHS

TOO BIG----) VIRUS---- DESKTOP----NOSE TOO

LARGE #### VIRUS selfless///SELFLESS ---

BODY NOT WHOLE---BODY AS PARTS ... Euripi-

des+++ No woman is a genius; *women are a decorative*

sex ++++ OSCAR WILDE #####*"If [women] become tired or even die, that does not matter. Let them die in childbirth–that is why they are there."++++MARTIN LUTHER* ------**"Woman is made to submit to man and to endure even injustice at his hands."Jean-Jacques Rousseau. "Women are nothing but machines for producing children – NAPOLEON ++++** " DESKTOP VIRUS**-3:16** *Unto the woman he said, I will greatly multiply thy sorrow and thy conception; in sorrow thou shalt bring forth children; and thy desire shall be to thy husband, and he shall rule over thee. The male is by nature superior and the female inferior, the male ruler and the female subject.* **OPEN----WOMEN FREE----NO LIMITS----VIRUS DESKTOP++Woman is a temple built over a sewer. –Tertullian ##### DESTROY ### VIRUS**-*---For it is improper for a woman to speak in an assembly, no matter what she says, even if she says admirable things, or even saintly things, that is of little consequence, since they come from the mouth of a woman. –Origen (d. 258): Fragments on First Corinthians.* ####**The feminist agenda is not about equal rights for women. It is about a socialist, anti-family political movement that encourages women to leave their husbands, kill their children, practice witchcraft, destroy capitalism and** become lesbians. — Pat Robertson, Southern Baptist leader 2:22 #Why exclude women? ...*Because their delicacy renders them unfit for practice and experience, in the great business of life, and the hardy enterprises of war, as well as the arduous cares of state. Besides, their attention is so much engaged with the necessary nurture of their children, that nature has made them fittest for domestic cares. John Adams (Women Have the Right to Work Wherever They Want, As Long As They Have the Dinner Ready When You Get Home John Wayne// ()* ##### Nature intended women to be our slaves... they are our property; we are not theirs. They belong to us, just as a tree that bears fruit belongs to a gardener...#Napoleon///= It is the law of nature that women should be held under the dominance of man.//{} *Confucius* <A proper wife should be as obedient as a slave Aristotle _____Men are governed by lines of intellect — women: by curves of emotion." James Joyce>?_*The education of women should always be relative to that of men. To please, to be useful to us, to make us love and esteem them, to educate us when young, to take care of us when grown up, to advise, to console us, to render our lives easy and agreeable....* #Rousseau "Finally — woman! ()One-half of mankind is weak, typically sick, changeable, inconstant — woman needs a religion of weakness that glorifies being weak, loving, being humbled as divine. "Friedrich Nietzsche

SMOKE started coming out of the machine and I quickly pulled out the board and tried to figure out the code to smash the glass ceiling as quickly as possible. The smoke made it harder and harder for me to see.

Code:

Preventing**BARRIER**Oppression**SMASH**4SO-CIAL**Poliitcal**ECONOMIC**Equality**INVISIBLE**Barri-er**SMASH**hierarchy-**CLIMB**high**ACHIEVING**woman

THE GLASS CEILING STARTED TO CRACK and I ran out of the basement and out of King Manu's bachelor pad. I made my way towards the Institution of Care and Preparation and there was a large crowd of people in front of the school, staring at a bunch of pink comets that were flying through the sky. Eivind, Dick and Billy were there wearing caps and gowns for the boys' graduation; so were Antonia and Penny; Mrs. Ruthberry and Mrs. Jackson and about two dozen armed General XY soldiers.

Billy spotted me near the school and yelled, "ALICE! Someone arrest her!" And just as he said the words, the ground beneath me started to shake and I fell on the floor. I looked up and saw an *enormous* shadow -- it was the

Shelatza Pink Dragon flying in the sky with Ayoka, Asais, Cheka and Jujuki riding on top of it. "Over here!" I yelled and moments later, the dragon slowly landed right in front of me. I pet it and it smiled. "Well done, Alice" Ayoka said, as she got off it.

"What the hell is going on?!" Billy yelled as he ran towards me, followed by a large crowd of people.

"What have you done now?" Eivind asked.

The crowd started opening up and a group of men were making their way towards us. It was King Manu and over two dozen armed General XY soldiers. King Manu looked at Ayoka in disbelief. "You're dead!" he said. "HOW CAN YOU BE IN MY TOWN?!" He forcefully grabbed her arm, but she pushed him off. "This isn't your town; the town belongs to the people."

King Manu grabbed a motor-weapon from General XY Harry and put it to Ayoka's head, while all of the General XY soldiers aimed their weapons at me, Asais, Cheka and Jujuki.

My heart was racing, but I was so furious I couldn't be scared. I closed my eyes and pictured King Manu unarmed and when I opened my eyes again, his motor weapon vanished as if into thin air. "WITCH!" he yelled at me. "SHE'S A WITCH! END THEM ALL!"

The Shelatza Pink Dragon looked enraged and her eyes had turned yellow. She took a deep breath and spit fire at the group of General XY soldiers standing in front of us, killing several of them instantly and injuring others.

But General XY Harry shot the Pink Dragon repeatedly from the roof of the Institution and she couldn't move. "NO!" I yelled, as the dragon shut her eyes. Several hundred General XY soldiers were running towards the school and towards us and they were armed with even larger motor weapons. "Turn yourself in!" Harry yelled. "Your time is over."

Ayoka, Cheka, Jujuki and I grabbed the weapons of the dead soldiers on the ground, but we were outnumbered badly. There was no way we were going to be able to take them all. I grabbed my portable computer and typed:

Code: **Motor-Weapons:**   SHUTDOWN   >
SHUTDOWN -- Shut off--*New World*

The General XY soldiers aimed their motor weapons at us and General XY Harry yelled, "Shoot!" They all fired, but nothing came out.

I pictured a wall between us and the General XY soldiers and a giant wall surfaced, blocking them from getting any closer to us. "WHOA!" Jujuki yelled. "THAT was cool!"

But I noticed I left King Manu on the opposite side of the wall, so I pictured him right in front of me and seconds later, there he was. "I KNEW YOU WERE A WITCH," he said. "ALL WOMEN ARE WITCHES!"

I aimed my motor weapon at King Manu and told him to go into the Institution of Care and Preparation. Eivind, Antonia, Billy, Dick and Penny looked on as I brought him into the school. "WTF is she doing?" Antonia asked.

I walked into the Mirror Room still pointing my motor weapon at King Manu. "I don't lose," King Manu told me. "I'm not supposed to lose." He SHOVED me to the ground and sent my motor weapon flying in the air. Then he grabbed me by the throat and was choking me using all of his strength. But I pictured a world without him and I grabbed his arm and removed it from my throat; then I pushed him as hard as I could into the 3rd mirror which instantly shattered, sending King Manu through the portal, to Shelatza. I immediately pictured the portal closed and it shut completely; the cracks disappearing in seconds.

Ayoka, Asais, Cheka and Jujuki ran into the classroom seconds after.. "Alice, are you OK?"

Penny followed them into the classroom. "What's going on, Alice? It's so scary out there -- I'm so wittle and so scared!" she said as she ate her goobers.

"Why are you so pinkish like?" Penny asked Ayoka. "I would give you some of my Goobers but they're only for wittle people like me. Hehe," she said.

Ayoka, Asais and Cheka looked at Penny, confused. "What the hell are you? What is that?" Cheka asked.

"She doesn't know anything about life," I explained. "We have to help her. She's a blank slate."

"This is worse than I thought," Ayoka said.

My mom walked into the mirror room accompanied by Mrs. Ruthberry, Mrs. Jackson; Mrs. Gilbert and Antonia and there was something very different about all of them -- for the first time ever, they looked...relieved. "Thank you, Alice," Mrs. Ruthberry said. "Thank you." My mother walked over to me and hugged me: "I'm proud of you, Alice," she said, something I had never heard my mother say in my entire life.

27

Pink Fraternité

We all joined hands in The Mirror Room for the first chapter in our her-story: Ayoka (our newly appointed Queen); Asais; Cheka, Jujuki; Penny; Antonia; Mrs. Gilbert; Mrs. Ruthberry; Mrs. Jackson and I. Eivind also came into the Mirror Room with Billy and Dick and watched as we signed and dated the Declaration of Equality Proclamation for all people. At last, women will be included in an important document.

"King Manu's decisions have hurt my people in more ways than one," Ayoka said. "We need a softer, nurturing hand to fix the problems and the messes he created. All citizens with be fully empowered participants and all will be equal," she said.

Eivind walked up to the podium and read the document:

DECLARATION OF EQUALITY PROCLAMATION:

"ALL MEN AND WOMEN ARE COMPLETELY AND TOTALLY EQUAL. EVERY SOUL HAS A RIGHT TO EQUALITY, LIBERTY AND LIFE UNDER THE LAW.

REGARDLESS OF RACE, GENDER, SEX OR ECONOMIC BACKGROUND.

Math EQUATION for equality;

f=m (AG) Brain F=Brain M _+SOUL F=SOUL M CITIZENSHIP F + CITIZENSHIP _EQUALITY (FEMALE ++++ MALE) SUBMITTED TO UNIVERSE. UNIVERSE PROVIDES EQ (Equilibrium)

I walked over to Eivind and he looked sad. "I'm sorry I hurt you, Alice. I shouldn't have done that," he said, sincerely. "I appreciate that Eivind," I said as I took my ring off my finger and gave it back to him. "I really do."

ABOUT THE AUTHOR

Laura Elizabeth Hernandez holds a
Bachelor's Degree in History and a Post-bac-
calaureate certificate in Education from
Ramapo College. She has written for
Cafemom's "The Stir," *The Huffington Post*,
Latina.com and *MamasLatinas.com*. Laura
began writing short stories and fiction at an
early age—winning a statewide Martin Luther
King Jr. Essay Contest and earning the "Eng-
lish" award at her elementary school's Eighth
Grade Graduation. She writes what she sees.
Readers can draw their own conclusions.
She lives in New Jersey and she loves it there.

Thank you to Lee Hernandez and Chet Kozlowski.

I want to thank God and of course my parents and my best friend Viviamna Grijalba.

God bless,
Laura

www.ingramcontent.com/pod-product-compliance
Lightning Source LLC
Chambersburg PA
CBHW071837020726
47502CB00004B/1392